RUMOURS ON THE RED CARPET

RUMOURS ON THE RED CARPET

BY

CAROLE MORTIMER

First published in Great Britain 2013
by Mills & Boon, an imprint of Harlequin (UK) Limited,
Large Print edition 2014
Eton House, 18-24 Paradise Road,
Richmond, Surrey, TW9 1SR

© 2013 Carole Mortimer

ISBN: 978 0 263 24039 9

Printed and bound in Great Britain
by CPI Antony Rowe, Chippenham, Wiltshire

Peter, as always.

CHAPTER ONE

'ENJOYING THE VIEW...?'

Thia tensed, a shiver of awareness quivering down the length of her spine at the sound of that deep voice coming out of the darkness behind her, before turning quickly to search those shadows for the man who had just spoken to her.

She was able to make out a tall figure in the moonlight just feet away from where she stood, alone on the balcony that surrounded the whole of this luxurious penthouse apartment on the fortieth floor of one of the impressive buildings lighting up the New York skyline. Only dim light spilled from the open French doors of the apartment further down the balcony—along with the sound of tinkling laughter and the chatter of the fifty or so party guests still inside—making it impossible for Thia to see any more than that the man was very tall, dark and broad-shouldered. Imposingly so.

Dangerously so…?

The wariness still humming through her body just at the sound of the deep and seductive timbre of his voice said a definite *yes!*

Thia's fingers tightened about the breast-high balustrade in front of her. 'I was, yes…' she answered pointedly.

'You're a Brit,' he observed deeply.

'From London,' Thia confirmed shortly, really hoping that he would take note of that terseness and leave her to her solitude.

The New York night skyline, amazing as it was, hadn't been Thia's main reason for coming outside into the balmy evening air fifteen minutes ago, when the other guests had all been preoccupied with their excitement at the late arrival of Lucien Steele, American zillionaire businessman, and the party's guest of honour. That so many high-profile actors, actresses and politicians had turned out for the event was indicative of the amount of power the man wielded.

After all Jonathan's hype about him Thia had

to admit that she hadn't found him so prepossessing—a man of middle age and average height, slightly stocky and balding. But maybe all that money and power made him more attractive? In any event, Thia had just been grateful that he had arrived at last—if only because it had allowed her to slip outside and *be* alone—instead of just *feeling* alone.

Thia certainly hadn't intended to find herself alone on the balcony with a man who exuded such an intensity of power and sexual attraction she could almost taste it...

'A Brit, from London, who's avoiding the party inside...?' that deep voice guessed with dry amusement.

Having been to three other parties just like this one in the four days since her arrival in New York, Thia had to admit to having become slightly bored—jaded?—by them. The first one had been fun—exciting, even—meeting people she had only ever seen on the big or little screen before, world-famous actors and actresses and high-profile politicians. But the artificiality of it was all becoming a bit samey now. The conversations were repetitive and too loud, the laughter even more so, with everyone seemingly out to impress or better everyone else, their excessive wealth literally worn on their sleeves.

This constant round of parties also meant that she'd had very little opportunity for any time or private conversation with Jonathan, the man she had come to New York to visit…

Jonathan Miller, the English star of *Network,* a new American thriller television series set in New York, directed by this evening's host, Felix Carew, and co-starring his young and sexy wife Simone as the love-interest.

The show had been an instant hit, and Jonathan was currently the darling of New York's beautiful people—and, as Thia had discovered these past four days, there were a *lot* of beautiful people in New York!

And not a single one of them had felt any qualms about ignoring the woman who had been seen at Jonathan's side on those evenings once they'd learnt that Thia was of no social or political value to them whatsoever.

Not that Thia minded being ignored. She had

very quickly discovered she had no more in common with New York's elite than they had with her.

She was pleased for Jonathan's success, of course. The two of them had known each other for a couple of years now, after meeting at the London restaurant where Thia always worked the late shift, leaving her free to attend her university course in the day.

She and Jonathan had met quite by chance, when he had been appearing in a play at the theatre across the street from the restaurant and had started calling in late in the evening a couple of times a week for something to eat, once the theatre had closed for the night.

They had chatted on those evenings, then dated casually for a few weeks. But there had been no spark between them and the relationship had quickly fallen into the 'just friends' category. Then, four months ago, Jonathan had landed the lead role in the television series over here, and Thia had accepted that even that friendship would be over once Jonathan moved to New York.

He had telephoned a couple of times in the

months that followed, just light and friendly conversations, when they had caught up on each other's lives, and then a month ago Jonathan had
flown back to England for the weekend, insisting
he had missed her and wanted to spend all his
time back home with her. And it had been fun.
Thia had arranged to have the weekend off so
that they could have dinner together in the evening, visits to museums and walks in the parks
during the day, before Jonathan had to fly back to
New York to start filming again on the Monday.

But no one had been more surprised than Thia
when a first-class plane ticket for a week-long
stay in New York had been delivered to her by
messenger just two days later!

She had telephoned Jonathan immediately, of
course, to tell him she couldn't possibly accept
such generosity from him. But he had insisted,
saying he could well afford it and, more to the
point, he wanted to see her again. He wanted to
show her New York, and for New York to see her.

Thia's pride had told her she should continue
to refuse, but Jonathan had been very persuasive,
and as she hadn't been able to afford a holiday

for years the temptation had just been too much. So she had accepted, with the proviso that he cancelled the first class ticket and changed it to a standard fare. Spending that amount of money on an airfare seemed obscene to her, in view of her own financial difficulties.

Jonathan had assured her that she would have her own bedroom in his apartment, and that he just wanted her to come and enjoy New York with him. She had even gone out and spent some of her hard-earned savings on buying some new clothes for the trip!

Except Jonathan's idea of her enjoying New York with him was vastly different from Thia's own. They had attended parties like this one every night, and Jonathan would sleep off the effects the following morning. Meanwhile his late afternoons and early evenings were usually spent secluded somewhere with Simone Carew, going over the script together.

Seeing so little of Jonathan during the day, and attending parties in the evenings, Thia had started to wonder why he had bothered to invite her here at all.

And she now found herself irritated that, once again, Jonathan had disappeared with Simone shortly after they had arrived at this party he had claimed was so important to him on account of the presence of Lucien Steele, the American billionaire owner of the television station responsible for *Network*. That desertion had left Thia being considered fair game by men like the one standing in the shadows behind her...

Well...perhaps not *exactly* like this man. The way he seemed to possess even the air about him told her that she had never met a man quite like this one before...

'Beautiful...' the man murmured huskily as he stepped forward to stand at the railing beside her.

Thia's heart skipped a beat, her nerve-endings going on high alert as her senses were instantly filled with the light smell of lemons—his cologne?—accompanied by an insidious maleness that she guessed was all him.

She turned to look at him, tilting her head back as she realised how much taller he was than her, even in her four-inch-heeled take-me-to-bed shoes. Taller, and so broad across the shoulders, with dark hair that rested low on the collar of his white shirt and black evening jacket. His face appeared to be all hard angles in the moonlight: strong jaw, chiselled lips, long aquiline nose, high cheekbones. And those pale and glittering eyes—

Piercing eyes, that she now realised were looking at *her* in admiration rather than at the New York skyline!

Thia repressed another quiver of awareness at having this man look at her so intently, realising that she was completely alone out here with a man she didn't know from—well, from Adam.

'Have they all stopped licking Lucien Steele's highly polished handmade Italian leather shoes yet, do you think?' she prompted in her nervousness, only to give a pained grimace at her uncharacteristic sharpness. 'I'm sorry—that was incredibly rude of me.' She winced, knowing how important Lucien Steele's goodwill was to Jonathan's success in the US. He had certainly emphasised it often enough on the drive over here!

'But true?' the man drawled dryly.

'Perhaps.' She nodded. 'But I'm sure that Mr

Steele has more than earned the adoration being showered upon him so effusively.'

Teeth gleamed whitely in the darkness as the man gave a hard and humourless smile. 'Or maybe he's just so rich and powerful no one has ever dared to tell him otherwise?'

'Maybe,' she conceded ruefully. 'Cynthia Hammond.' She thrust out her hand in an effort to bring some normality to this conversation. 'But everyone calls me Thia.'

He took possession of her hand—there was no other way to describe the way the paleness of her hand just disappeared inside the long bronzed strength of his. And Thia could not ignore the jolt of electricity zinging along her fingers and arm at contact with the warmth of his skin...

'I've never been particularly fond of being a part of what everyone else does,' he murmured throatily. 'So I think I'll call you Cyn...'

Just the way he said that word, in that deliciously deep and sexy voice, was enough to send yet more shivers of awareness down Thia's spine. Her breasts tingled with that awareness, the nipples puckering to tight and sensitive berries as they pressed against the sheer material of the clinging blue ankle-length gown she wore.

And it was a totally inappropriate reaction to a complete stranger!

Jonathan might have done yet another disappearing act with Simone forty minutes ago, but that certainly didn't mean Thia was going to stand here and allow herself to be seduced by some dark-haired hunk, who looked sinfully delicious in his obviously expensive evening suit but so far hadn't even been polite enough to introduce himself!

'And you are...?'

Those teeth gleamed even whiter in the darkness as he gave a wolfish smile. 'Lucien Steele.'

Thia gave a snort. 'I don't think so!' she scoffed.

'No?' He sounded amused by her scepticism.

'No,' she repeated decisively.

He raised one dark brow. 'Why not?'

She breathed her impatience. 'Well, for one thing you aren't nearly old enough to be the self-made zillionaire Lucien Steele.' She estimated this man was aged somewhere in his early to mid-thirties, ten or twelve years older than her own twenty-three, and she knew from the things Jonathan had told her about this evening's guest of honour that Lucien Steele had not only been the richest man in New York for the last ten years, but was also the most powerful.

He gave an unconcerned shrug of those impossibly wide shoulders. 'What can I say? My parents were wealthy to begin with, and I'd made my own first million by the time I was twenty-one.'

'Also,' Thia continued, determined, 'I saw Mr Steele when he arrived.'

It had been impossible to miss the awed reaction of the other guests. Those incredibly rich and beautiful people had all, without exception, fallen absolutely silent the moment Lucien Steele had appeared in the doorway. And Felix Carew, a powerful man in his own right, had become almost unctuous as he moved swiftly across the room to greet his guest.

Thia gave a rueful shake of her head. 'Lucien Steele is in his early forties, several inches shorter than you are, and stocky, with a shaved head.' In fact on first glance she had thought the man more resembled a thug rather than the richest and most powerful man in New York!

'That would be Dex.'

'Dex...?' she echoed doubtfully.

'Mmm.' The man beside her nodded unconcernedly. 'He takes his duties as my bodyguard very seriously—to the point that he always insists upon entering a room before I do. I'm not sure why,' he mused. 'Perhaps he expects there to be an assassin on the other side of every door...'

Thia felt a sinking sensation in the pit of her stomach as she heard the amused dismissal in this man's—in Lucien Steele's?—voice. Moistening her lips with the tip of tongue before speaking, she said, 'And where is Dex now...?'

'Probably standing guard on the other side of those French doors.' He nodded down the balcony to the same doorway Thia had escaped through minutes ago.

And was Dex making sure that no one came outside, or was he ensuring that Thia couldn't return inside until this man wished her to...?

She gave another frown as she looked up searchingly at the man now standing so near to her she could feel the heat emanating from his body on the bareness of her shoulders and arms. Once again she took note of that inborn air of power, arrogance, she had sensed in him from the first.

For all the world as if he was *used* to people licking his highly polished handmade Italian leather shoes...

Lucien continued to hold Cyn's now trembling hand and waited in silence for her to gather her breath as she looked up at him between long and silky lashes with eyes a dark and mysterious cobalt blue.

Those eyes became shadowed with apprehension as she gave another nervous flick of her little pink tongue over the moist fullness of her perfectly shaped lips. 'The same Lucien Steele who owns Steele Technology, Steele Media, Steele Atlantic Airline *and* Steele Industries, as well as all those other Steele Something-or-Others?' she murmured faintly.

He shrugged. 'It seemed like a good idea to diversify.'

She determinedly pulled her hand from his grasp before tightly gripping the top of the balustrade. 'The same Lucien Steele who's a zillionaire?'

'I believe you said that already...' Lucien nodded.

She drew in a deep breath, obviously completely unaware of how it tightened the material of her dress across her breasts and succeeded in outlining the fullness of those—aroused?—nipples. Nipples that were a delicate pink or a succulent rose? Whatever their colour, he was sure they would taste delicious. Sweet and juicy, and oh so ripe and responsive as he licked and suckled them.

He had noticed the woman he now knew to be Cynthia Hammond the moment he'd entered Felix and Simone Carew's penthouse apartment a short time ago. It had been impossible not to as she'd stood alone at the back of the opulent room, her hair a sleek and glossy unadorned black as it fell silkily to just below her shoulders, her eyes that deep cobalt blue in the beautiful pale delicacy of her face.

She wore a strapless ankle-length gown of that same deep blue, leaving the tops of her breasts, shoulders and arms completely bare. The smoothness of her skin was a beautiful pearly white unlike any other Lucien had ever seen: a pale ivory tinted lightly pink, luminescent. Smoothly delicate and pearly skin his fingers itched to touch and caress.

The simple style of that silky blue gown allowed it to cling to every curvaceous inch of her full breasts, slender waist and gently flaring hips, so much so that Lucien had questioned whether or not she wore anything beneath it.

He still questioned it...

But what had really made him take notice of her, even more than her natural beauty or the pearly perfection of her skin, was the fact that instead of moving towards him, as every other person in the room had done, this pale and delicately beautiful woman had instead taken advantage of his arrival to slip quietly from the room and go outside onto the balcony.

Nor had she returned by the time Lucien had finally managed to extract himself from the—

what had she called it a few moments ago? The licking of his 'highly polished handmade Italian leather shoes'. His curiosity piqued—and very little piqued his jaded palate nowadays!—Lucien hadn't been able to resist coming out onto the balcony to look for her the moment he had managed to escape all that cloying attention.

She drew in another deep breath now before speaking, causing the fullness of her breasts to once again swell deliciously over the bodice of that clinging blue gown.

'I really do apologise for my rudeness, Mr Steele. It's no excuse, but I'm really not having a good evening—and my rudeness to you means that it has just got so much worse!' she conceded with another pained wince. 'But that is really no reason for me to have been rude about you—or to you.'

He quirked one dark brow. 'I don't think you know me well enough *as yet* to speak with any authority on whether or not I *deserve* for you to be rude to me or about me,' he drawled mockingly.

'Well...no...' She was obviously slightly un-

nerved by his emphasis on the words 'as yet'...
'But—' She gave a shake of her head, causing
that silky and completely straight black hair to
glide across the bareness of her shoulders and caress tantalisingly across the tops of her breasts.
'I still shouldn't have been so outspoken about
someone I only know about from the media.'

'Especially when we all know how inaccurate
the media can be?' he drawled wryly.

'Exactly!' She nodded enthusiastically before
just as quickly pausing to eye him uncertainly.
'Don't you own something like ninety per cent
of the worldwide media?'

'That would be contrary to monopoly regulations,' he drawled dismissively.

'Do zillionaires bother with little things like
regulations?' she teased.

He chuckled huskily. 'They do if they don't
want their zillionaire butts to end up in court!'

Thia felt what was becoming a familiar quiver
down the length of her spine at the sound of this
man's throaty laughter. As she also acknowledged that, for all this man unnerved her, she

was actually enjoying herself—possibly for the first time since arriving in New York.

'Are you cold?'

Thia had no chance to confirm or deny that she was before Lucien Steele removed his evening jacket and placed it about the bareness of her shoulders. It reached almost down to her knees and smelt of the freshness of those lemons as his warmth surrounded her, and of the more insidious and earthy smell of the man himself.

'No, really—'

'Leave it.' Both his hands came down onto the shoulders of the jacket as she would have reached up and removed it.

Thia shivered anew as she felt the warmth of those long and elegant hands even through the material of his jacket. A shiver entirely due to the presence of this overwhelming man—also the reason for her earlier shiver—rather than any chill in the warm evening air...

His hands left her shoulders reluctantly as he moved to stand beside her once again, that pale gaze—silver?—once again intent on her face. The snug fit of his evening shirt revealed that his shoulders really were that wide, his chest muscled, his waist slender above lean hips and long legs; obviously Lucien Steele didn't spend *all* of his days sitting in boardrooms and adding to his billions.

'Why aren't you having a good evening?' he prompted softly.

Why? Because this visit to New York hadn't turned out to be anything like Thia had imagined it would be. Because she had once again been brought to a party and then quickly abandoned by—well, Jonathan certainly wasn't her boyfriend, but she had certainly thought of him as a friend. A friend who had disappeared with their hostess within minutes of their arrival, leaving her to the untender mercies of New York's finest.

Latterly she wasn't having a good evening because she was far too aware of the man standing beside her—of the way the warmth and seductive smell of Lucien Steele's tailored jacket made her feel as if she was surrounded by the man himself.

And lastly because Thia had no idea how to

deal with the unprecedented arousal now coursing through her body!

She gave a shrug. 'I don't enjoy parties like
this one.'

'Why not?'

She grimaced, taking care not to insult this
man for a second time this evening. 'It's just a
personal choice.'

He nodded. 'And where do you fit in with this
crowd? Are you an actress?'

'Heavens, no!'

'A wannabe?'

'I beg your pardon...?'

He shrugged those impossibly wide shoulders.
'Do you wannabe an actress?'

'Oh, I see.' Thia gave a rueful smile. 'No, I
have no interest in becoming an actress, either.'

'A model?'

She snorted. 'Hardly, when I'm only five feet
two inches in my bare feet!'

'You aren't being very helpful, Cyn.' There
was an underlying impatience in that amused
tone. Thia had seen far too much of the reaction of New York's elite these past four days not

to know they had absolutely no interest in culti-
vating the company of a student and a waitress.
Lucien Steele would have no further interest in
her, either, once he knew. Which might not be a
bad thing…

Her chin rose determinedly. 'I'm just a nobody
on a visit to New York.'

Lucien totally disagreed with at least part of
that statement. Cynthia Hammond was certainly
somebody. Somebody—a woman—whose beauty
and conversation he found just as intriguing as
he had hoped he might…

She quirked dark brows. 'I believe that's your
cue to politely excuse yourself?'

His eyes narrowed. 'And why would I wish to
do that?'

She shrugged her shoulders beneath his jacket.
'It's what everyone else I've met in New York has
done once they realise I'm of use to them.'

Yes, Lucien could imagine, knowing New York
society as well as he did, that its members would
have felt no hesitation whatsoever in making their
lack of interest known. 'I believe I've already
stated that I prefer not to be like everyone else.'

'Ain't that the truth? I mean—' A delicious blush now coloured those pale ivory cheeks as she briefly closed her eyes before looking up at him apologetically. 'I apologise once again. I'm really *not* having a good evening!' She sighed.

He nodded. 'Would you like to leave? We could go somewhere quiet and have a drink together?'

Cyn blinked those long lashes. 'I beg your pardon...?'

Lucien gave a hard, humourless smile. 'I hate parties like this one too.'

'But you're the guest of honour!'

He grimaced. 'I especially hate parties where I'm the guest of honour.'

Thia looked up at him searchingly, not sure whether or not Lucien Steele was playing with her. Not sure why he was bothering, if that should be the case!

The steady regard of those pale eyes and the grimness of his expression told her that this was a man who rarely, if ever, played.

He was seriously asking her to leave the Carews' party with him...

CHAPTER TWO

THIA GAVE A rueful shake of her head as she smiled. 'That really wouldn't be a good idea.'

'Why not?'

'Are you always this persistent?' She frowned.

He seemed to give the idea some thought before answering. 'When I want something badly enough, yes,' he finally murmured, without apology.

The intensity in that silver gaze as he looked down at Thia told her all too clearly that right now Lucien Steele wanted *her*.

Badly.

Wickedly!

She repressed another shiver of awareness just at the thought of how those chiselled lips and strong hands might feel as they sought out all the secret dips and hollows of her body.

'I really think it's time I went back inside.' She was slightly flustered as she slipped his jacket from about her shoulders and held it out to him. 'Please take it,' she urged when he made no effort to do so.

He looked down at her searchingly for several seconds before slowly taking the jacket and placing it dismissively over the balustrade in front of him—as if it *hadn't* cost as much as Thia might earn in a year as a waitress including tips!

'Cyn...'

He wasn't even touching her, and yet he managed to hold her mesmerised just by the way he murmured his own unique name for her in that deeply seductive voice, sending more rivulets of awareness down Thia's spine and causing a return of that tingling sensation in her breasts, accompanied by an unaccustomed warmth between her thighs.

'Yes...?' she answered breathlessly.

'I *really* want you to leave with me.'

'I can't.' She groaned in protest at the compulsion in the huskiness of his voice, sure that this man—a man who was not only sinfully handsome but rich as Creosus—rarely, if ever, asked for anything from anyone. He just took.

'Why not?'

'I just— What colour are your eyes, exactly…?' Whatever colour they were, they held Thia captive by their sheer intensity!

He blinked at the unexpectedness of the question. 'My eyes…?'

'Yes.'

His mouth twisted in a rueful smile. 'I believe it says grey on my passport.'

Thia gave a shake of her head. 'They're silver,' she corrected, barely able to breathe now, even knowing this was madness—that she was so totally aware of Lucien Steele, her skin so sensitised by the intensity of that glittering silver gaze fixed on her so intently, that she could feel the brush of each individual strand of her hair as it caressed lightly, silkily, across her shoulders and the tops of her breasts.

A totally unexpected and unprecedented reaction. To any man. Goodness knew Jonathan was handsome enough, with his overlong blond hair, laughing blue eyes and lean masculinity, but for some reason she had just never found him attractive in *that* way. Just looking at Lucien Steele, knowing she was aware of everything about him, of all that underlying and leashed power, she knew that she never would be attracted to Jonathan—that Lucien Steele was so overpowering he ruined a woman's appreciation for any other man.

'Grey…silver…they can be whatever the hell colour you want them to be if you'll only leave with me now,' Lucien Steele urged again, with that same intensity.

She was tempted—Lord, was Thia tempted!— but it wouldn't do. No matter how distracted and inattentive Jonathan might choose to be, she couldn't arrive at a party with him and then leave with another man. Especially a man she found as disturbing as she did Lucien Steele!

A man who was over six feet of lean and compelling muscle. A man who was too handsome for his own good. A man who was just too…too intense—too much of everything—and whom she had discovered she found so mouthwateringly tempting.

Thia straightened her spine determinedly. 'I came here with someone.'

Those silver eyes narrowed with displeasure. 'A male someone?'

'Yes.'

His gaze moved to her left hand. 'You aren't wearing any rings.'

Thia gave a shake of her head. 'He isn't that sort of friend.'

'Then who is he?'

'I don't think that's any of your business—'

'And if I choose to make it so?'

'He's just a friend,' she dismissed impatiently, not sure even that was true any longer. Jonathan had made it obvious he inhabited a different world from her now—a world she had no inclination or desire ever to become a part of.

Lucien Steele's expression was grim as he shook his head. 'He can't be that much of a friend if he brought you here and then just left you to your own devices.'

This was the same conclusion Thia had come to over the past four days! 'I'm an adult and perfectly capable of looking after myself, thank you very much,' she assured him tartly.

Lucien Steele raised dark brows. 'So much so

that you came out here alone rather than remain at the party?'

She felt stung by the mockery in his tone. 'Maybe I just wanted to get away from all that boot-licking?' she challenged.

'Handmade Italian leather shoes,' he corrected dryly.

'Whatever,' Thia dismissed impatiently. 'I'm sure you didn't come here alone tonight, either...' She vaguely recalled Jonathan mentioning something about Lucien Steele currently being involved with the supermodel Lyndsay Turner. A woman who, six feet tall and blond, couldn't be any more Thia's opposite!

Lucien's mouth thinned as he recalled the scene that had taken place with Lyndsay a week ago. A scene in which the supermodel had seriously overestimated his feelings for her and that had resulted in the end of their month-long relationship. Hell, he didn't *do* promises—let alone engagement and wedding rings.

He grimaced. 'As it happens, I did. And I want to leave with *you*,' he added determinedly, knowing it had been a long time since he had wanted anything as much as he now wanted to spend time alone with Cynthia Hammond.

'You don't know the first thing about me,' she dismissed exasperatedly.

'Which is precisely the reason I want the two of us to go somewhere quiet and talk—so that I can get to know you better,' he pushed insistently. The more this woman resisted him the more determined he became to leave the party with her this evening. At which time he intended to find out exactly which of Felix Carew's male guests was the friend Cyn had mentioned...

She attempted to tease. 'Has no one ever told you that it isn't possible to have *everything* you want?'

'No.' A nerve pulsed in Lucien's tightly clenched jaw.

'Because you're so rich and powerful no one would ever dare to tell you otherwise?' she asked softly, reminding him of his earlier comment.

'No doubt.' Again he answered unapologetically.

Thia gave an exasperated laugh at this man's unrelenting arrogance; she really had never met a man quite like him before! 'Then I shall have the distinction of being the first to do so! It's been...*interesting* meeting you, Mr Steele, but I really should go back inside and— What are you doing...?' She gasped softly as his gaze continued to hold hers captive even as his head slowly descended towards her, the warmth of his breath as light as a caress against her cheeks and lips.

'I want—I'd *like* to kiss you,' he corrected huskily, his lips just centimetres away from her own. 'Are you going to let me?'

'No...' Thia was aware her protest sounded half-hearted and she found herself unable to look away from those mesmerising silver eyes.

'Say yes, Cyn.' He moved slightly, his lips a hot and brief caress against the heat of her cheek before he raised his head and looked at her once again, not touching her with anything but the intensity of that glittering gaze.

She couldn't breathe, couldn't move so much as a muscle, as she continued to be held captive by the intensity of those eyes. Much like a deer caught in the headlights of an oncoming car. Or a freight train. Either of which was capable of flattening whatever stood in their way. As Lucien Steele's brand of seduction was capable of crushing both Thia and her resistance...

She drew in a shaky breath before stepping back and away from him. 'Thank you for the invitation, Mr Steele, but no.'

'Lucien.'

She shook her head. 'I believe I would prefer to continue calling you Mr Steele. Not that we'll ever meet again after this evening. But even so—'

'Why not?'

Thia gave a lightly dismissive laugh at the sharpness of his tone. 'Because you inhabit this world and I—I inhabit another one.'

'And yet here you are...?'

'Yes, here I am.' And she wouldn't be coming back again if she could help it! 'I really do have to go back inside now—'

'And look for your *friend?*' he prompted harshly.

'Yes.' Thia grimaced, very much afraid that she and that 'friend' were going to have words before the evening was over. Certainly she had no intention of letting Jonathan get away with bringing her to another party like this one and then leaving her to go off somewhere with the beautiful Simone. Jonathan's habit of just forgetting Thia's existence the moment they arrived at one of these parties was becoming tedious as well as a complete waste of her time, when she really didn't enjoy being here.

'Who is he?'

'It's really none of your business,' Thia snapped in irritation at Lucien Steele's persistence.

Those silver eyes narrowed, his jaw tightening. 'At least tell me where you're staying in New York.'

She gave an exasperated grimace. 'That's even less your business! Now, if you'll excuse me...' Thia didn't wait for him to reply before turning on her four-inch-heeled shoes and walking away, her head held determinedly high as she forced herself not to hurry, not to reveal how desperately she needed to get away from Lucien Steele's disturbingly compelling presence.

Even if she *was* completely aware of that silver gaze as a sensual caress across the bareness of her shoulders and down the length of her spine and the slender curve of her hips!

Lucien Steele was without doubt the most disturbingly sexual man she had ever—

'Where the *hell* have you been?' Jonathan demanded the moment she stepped back into the Carews' huge sitting room. The expression on his boyishly handsome face was accusing as he took a rough hold of her arm.

An entirely unfair accusation, in Thia's estimation, considering *he* was the one who had gone missing with their hostess for almost an hour, leaving her to be approached by Lucien Steele!

'Can we talk about this somewhere less…public, Jonathan?' She glared at him, very aware of the silent—listening?—presence of Lucien Steele's bodyguard, Dex, just feet away from the two of them. 'Preferably in the privacy of your car, once we've *left,*' she added pointedly.

Jonathan looked less than pleased by her last comment. 'You know damned well I can't leave yet,' he dismissed impatiently, even as he physically dragged her over to a quieter corner of the room.

'Could that possibly be because you haven't yet had a chance to say hello to Lucien Steele?' Thia felt stung into taunting him as she rubbed the top of her arm where Jonathan's fingers had dug so painfully into her flesh that she would probably have bruises to show for it tomorrow. 'I noticed you and our beautiful hostess were noticeably absent when he arrived.'

'What does *that* mean?' he glowered darkly. 'And what the hell's got into you, talking to me like that?'

'Nothing's got into me.' She gave a weary sigh, knowing that not all of her frustration with this evening was Jonathan's fault. Her nerves were still rattled from that encounter with Lucien Steele on the balcony—to a degree that she could still feel the seductive brush of those chiselled lips against her cheek and the warmth of his breath brushing against her skin... 'I just want to leave, that's all.' She grimaced.

'I've told you that I can't go just yet.' Jonathan scowled down at her.

'Then I'll just have to go downstairs and get a taxi—'

'It's a cab,' he corrected impatiently. 'And you aren't going anywhere until I say you can,' he added determinedly.

Thia looked at him searchingly, noting the reckless brightness of his eyes and the unaccustomed flush to his cheeks. 'Have you been drinking...?'

'It's a party. Of course I've been drinking!' Jonathan eyed her impatiently.

'In that case I'm definitely taking a cab back to your apartment,' Thia stated firmly.

'I said you'll leave when I *say* you can!' His eyes glittered.

Thia's cheeks warmed as she stared at him incredulously. 'Who do you think you are to talk to me like that?' she gasped.

Jonathan's expression darkened. 'I think I'm the man who paid for you to come to New York!'

Her eyes widened incredulously. 'And you believe that gives you the right to tell me what I can and can't do?'

'I think it gives me the right to do with you whatever the hell I feel like doing!' he sneered.

Thia felt the colour drain from her cheeks at the unmistakable threat in his voice. 'I don't know what's got into you, Jonathan.' Her voice shook as she tried to hold back tears of hurt. 'But I do know I don't like you like this. You're obviously drunk. Or something.' She wasn't a hundred per cent certain that reckless brightness in his eyes and the flush to his cheeks had been caused by alcohol alone...

Jonathan certainly wasn't behaving this evening—hadn't been for the past four days, if she was completely honest—like the charming and uncomplicated friend she had known in England...

She drew in a deep breath. 'I think it's best if I leave now, Jonathan. We can talk later. Or tomorrow—'

'You're staying put, damn it.' He reached out and grasped the top of her arm once again, the fingers of his other hand like a vice about her wrist as he twisted painfully.

Thia gave a gasp at the pain he was deliberately—viciously—inflicting on both her arm and her wrist. 'You're hurting me, Jonathan,' she breathed, very much aware of the other guests in the room and the curious sideways glances that were now being sent their way.

'Then stop being so damned difficult! I've said you aren't going anywhere and that's an end to it—' Jonathan broke off abruptly, his gaze moving past Thia and over her left shoulder and his eyes widening before he abruptly released her arm and wrist and forced a charmingly boyish smile to his lips.

Thia's spine stiffened as she guessed from the sudden pause in the conversation around them, the expectant stillness in the air and the way her skin tingled in awareness, exactly who was standing behind her.

Only one man had the power to cause such awe in New York's elite and the ability to possess the very air about him...

The same man who exuded such sexual attraction that it caused every nerve-ending in Thia's body to react and strain towards the pull of that raw sensuality!

Lucien Steele...

Lucien had remained out on the balcony for several more minutes after Cynthia Hammond had walked away from him, giving the hardness of his arousal time to subside even as he pondered the unexpected fierceness of his physical reaction to her.

Her skin—that pearly, luminescent skin—had been as soft and perfect to the light caress of his lips against her cheek as he had imagined it would be, and he could still smell her perfume... something lightly floral along with underlying warmly desirable woman. The same warmth that had surrounded him, enveloped him, as he'd shrugged back into his evening jacket ready for returning to the Carews' party as if the woman herself were wrapped around him.

Lucien couldn't remember the last time he'd had such a visceral reaction to a woman that he wanted to take her right here and right now. If he ever had...

All the more surprising because Cynthia Hammond, at little over five feet tall, ebony-haired and probably only twenty or so, wasn't the type of woman he usually found himself attracted to. He had always preferred tall, leggy blondes, and women nearer to his own age of thirty-five. Women who knew and accepted that his interest in them was purely physical, and that it would be fleeting.

Cynthia Hammond looked too young, too inexperienced to accept the intensity of passion Lucien would demand from her even for the brief time that his interest lasted. And it would be brief—a week or two, a month at the most—before Lucien once again found himself feeling restless, bored with having the same woman in his bed.

No, better by far, he had decided, that he stay well away from the too-young and too-inexperienced Cynthia Hammond.

And he would have done so if, when he had finally stepped back into the Carews' apartment, Dex hadn't felt it necessary to take him to one side and inform him of the way Jonathan Miller had verbally berated Cynthia Hammond the moment she'd returned to the party, before physically dragging her away.

Did that mean that Jonathan Miller, the star of one of the television series currently airing on Lucien's own network, was the friend Cyn had come to the party with?

Watching the couple as they'd stood together on the opposite side of the room, talking softly but obviously heatedly, Lucien had been unable to stop the narrowing of his eyes when he saw the way Cyn suddenly paled. His fists had clenched at his sides as he'd realised that Miller had a painful grip on her arm and his other hand was twisting her wrist, despite Cyn's obvious efforts to free herself. The thought of a single bruise marring the pearly perfection of her skin had been enough to send Lucien striding forcefully across the room.

Jonathan Miller was one of the reasons Lucien was back in New York at the moment. The actor's behaviour this past few months had become a definite cause for concern and required that Lucien intervene personally after receiving information that the verbal warning he had given Miller six weeks ago, about his drug habit and the affair he was having with his married co-star—the wife of the show's director—had made little difference to the other man's behaviour.

Another private meeting with Jonathan Miller would have to wait until tomorrow. At the moment Lucien was more concerned with the aggressive way the younger man was currently behaving towards Cyn. No matter how intense or demanding Lucien's own physical needs might be, he would never deliberately hurt a woman— he much preferred to give pleasure rather than pain—and he wouldn't tolerate another man behaving in that way in his presence, either.

His gaze settled on Cyn as she stood with her bared shoulders turned towards him. 'Are you ready to leave now…?' he prompted huskily.

Thia's heart leapt into her throat as Lucien Steele reiterated his invitation to leave the party with him, as he offered to take her away from this nightmare. Away from Jonathan. A Jonathan who was becoming unrecognisable as the charming man she had met two years ago—a man she had thought was her friend.

But friends didn't deliberately hurt each other, and the top of her arm still ached from where Jonathan's fingers had dug so painfully into her flesh just seconds ago, and her wrist was sore from where he had twisted it so viciously. Not only had he hurt her, but he had frightened her too when he had spoken to her so threateningly. And it shamed her, embarrassed her, to think that Lucien Steele might have witnessed that physical and verbal attack.

'Cyn...?'

She could see the confusion in Jonathan's eyes and he was the one to answer the other man lightly. 'I think you've made a mistake, Mr Steele. This is Thia Hammond, my—'

'Cyn...?'

Long, elegant fingers slipped possessively, gently beneath her elbow and Lucien Steele continued to ignore the other man as he came to stand beside her. Thia felt that now familiar shiver down the length of her spine just at the touch of those possessive fingers against her skin, accompanied by the compulsion in Lucien Steele's husky voice. She could actually *feel* that compulsion as that voice willed her to look up at him.

She turned slowly, much like a marionette whose strings were being pulled, her lids widening, pupils expanding, and all the air suddenly sucked from her lungs as she took her first clear look at Lucien Steele in the glare of light from the chandeliers above them.

Oh. My. God.

She had thought him mesmerising, compelling, as they had stood outside together in the moonlight, but that was as nothing compared to the intensity of the magnetism he exuded in the brightly lit sitting room of the Carews' apartment. So much so that even this huge room, the size of a tennis court, seemed too small to hold all that raw and savage power.

His hair was so deep a black it appeared almost blue beneath the lights of the chandelier, and his bronzed face was beautifully sculptured. His high, intelligent brow, the sharp blade of a nose between high cheekbones, and his mouth—oh, God, his mouth!—were sinfully, decadently chiseled. His top lip was slightly fuller than the bottom—an indication of the sensuality he had exuded when they were outside together on the balcony?—and his jaw was square and determined, darkened by the shadow of a dark stubble.

It was the face of a warrior, a marauder, a man

who took what he wanted and to hell with whoever or whatever stood in his way.

As if that savagely beautiful face wasn't enough,
his perfectly tailored evening suit—had Thia *really* had that gorgeous jacket wrapped about her
just minutes ago?—and white silk shirt showed
the perfection of his widely muscled shoulders
and chest, his tapered waist, powerful thighs and
long, lean legs encased in matching black trou-
sers above those soft Italian leather shoes she had
referred to so scathingly such a short time ago.

All the trappings of urbanity, in fact—an urbanity that was dispelled the moment she looked
at that handsomely savage face!

A face that was dominated by those amazing
and compelling silver eyes surrounded by long
and silky dark lashes.

Those same compelling silver eyes now held
Thia's own gaze captive, hostage, and refused to
release her until she acquiesced, surrendered to
that raw and demanding power...

CHAPTER THREE

'CYN...?' LUCIEN QUESTIONED for the third and last time—and that was twice more than he would have allowed any other woman.

If Cyn Hammond ignored him for a third time then he would take it that she was a willing participant in Miller's abusive treatment. It wasn't to Lucien's personal taste, but that was Cyn's business—not his. No matter how much he might desire her himself...

'Thia?' Jonathan Miller looked totally confused by this whole encounter.

Lucien's eyes moved past Cyn to the other man, hardening to steel as he pinned Miller with his razor-sharp gaze. Bruises were already forming on Cyn's arm where Miller had held her too tightly just minutes ago, and her wrist looked red and sore. An unforgivable assault, as far as

Lucien was concerned, on the perfection of that pearly unblemished skin.

'You hurt her, Miller,' he rasped harshly, his own fingers curling reassuringly about Cyn's elbow as he felt the way she still trembled. An indication that she really *wasn't* happy about Miller's rough treatment of her...

The other man's face flushed with anger—an emotion he quickly masked behind the boyishly charming smile that was currently holding American television audiences so enrapt, but succeeded only in leaving Lucien cold.

'Thia and I have had a slight misunderstanding, that's all—'

'It was *your* misunderstanding, Jonathan, not mine.' Cyn was the one to answer coldly and Lucien felt her straighten determinedly. 'Mr Steele has very kindly offered to drive me home, and I've decided to accept his offer.'

There were two things wrong with that statement as far as Lucien was concerned. One, he knew he was far from kind. Two, he had offered to take Cyn for a drink somewhere quieter than the Carews' apartment—not to drive her home.

Especially if that 'home' should also happen to be Miller's apartment...

But the details could be sorted out later. For the moment Lucien just wanted to get Cyn away from here. He could still feel the slight trembling of her slender but curvaceous body. Those cobalt blue eyes were dark, there was an enticing flush to her cheeks, her pouting lips were moist and parted, and those deliciously full breasts were once again swelling temptingly against the bodice of her gown as she breathed.

And Lucien could think of a much better use for all that pent up emotion than anger...

'How do the two of you even know each other?' Jonathan Miller scowled darkly.

'If you'll excuse us, Miller?' Lucien didn't spare the other man so much as a glance, let alone answer him, as he turned to give Dex a slight nod of his head. He held Cyn to his side by a light but firm grasp of her elbow as he walked away, the other guests immediately clearing a pathway for them to cross the room to the Carews' private elevator in the hallway.

'What the hell is going on—?'

Lucien gave a cold smile of satisfaction as he heard Miller's protest cut short, knowing that Dex would have responded to his silent instruction and, in his own inimitable and deadly style, prevented the actor from attempting to follow the two of them. Lucien's smile hardened, his eyes chilling to ice as he thought of the conversation he was going to have with Jonathan Miller tomorrow. A conversation that would now include a discussion on the other man's treatment of the delicately lovely woman at his side...

Thia had no idea what she was doing, agreeing to leave the Carews' party with the dangerously compelling Lucien Steele, of all people. Especially when he had made his physical interest in her so obvious during the time the two of them had been outside on the balcony together!

She just wanted to get away from here. From a Jonathan she no longer recognised. And from the curious glances of all the other guests as they observed the tension between the three of them—some surreptitiously, some blatantly.

But was leaving with the dangerously attractive Lucien Steele, a man who was so arrogant she wasn't sure she even liked him, really the answer…?

'Shouldn't we say goodbye to the Carews before we leave?' she prompted hesitantly as Lucien Steele pressed a button and the lift doors opened.

'Dex will deal with it,' he dismissed unconcernedly.

'I—then shouldn't we at least wait for him…?' Thia made no move to enter the lift, her nervousness increasing the longer she spent in this man's compelling company.

'He'll make his own way down.' Lucien Steele released her elbow as he indicated she should enter the lift ahead of him.

Thia still hesitated. She wanted to get away from Jonathan, yes, but she now realised she felt no safer with Lucien Steele—if for a totally different reason!

'Changed your mind…?' he drawled mockingly.

Her chin rose at the taunt. 'No.' She stepped determinedly into the lift, her gaze averted as

Lucien Steele stepped in beside her and pressed the button for the mirror-walled lift to descend.

Thia shot him several nervous glances from beneath her lashes as he stood broodingly on the other side of the lift, feeling that now familiar quiver trembling down her spine as she found herself surrounded by numerous mirrored images of him. This man was impressive under any circumstances, but she stood no chance of remaining immune to him in the confines of a lift.

Lucien Steele was sin incarnate, right from the top of his glossy hair—so much blacker than Thia's own, like shiny blue-black silk, the sort of tousled, overlong hair that made Thia's fingers itch to thread their way through it—to the soles of those Italian leather shoes.

He was a man so totally out of Thia's league that she had no business being there with him at all, let alone imagining threading her fingers through that delicious blue-black hair.

'Ask.'

Thia's startled gaze moved from that silky dark hair to the sculptured perfection of his face. Once again she felt that jolt of physical awareness as she found herself ensnared by the piercing intensity of those silver eyes. 'Um—sorry?'

He shrugged. 'You have a question you want to ask me.'

'I do…?'

His mouth twisted ruefully. 'You do.'

She chewed briefly on her bottom lip. 'Your hair—it's beautiful. I—I've never seen hair quite that blue-black colour before…?'

He raised a brow equally as dark. 'Are you sure you want *that* to be your one question?'

Thia blinked. 'My one question?'

He gave an abrupt inclination of his head. 'Yes.'

She frowned slightly. Surely he wasn't serious…? 'I've just never seen hair that colour before…' she repeated nervously. 'It's the colour of a starless night sky.'

His mouth twisted derisively. 'That was a statement, not a question.'

Yes, it was. But this man unnerved Thia to such a degree she couldn't think straight.

Lucien Steele sighed. 'Somewhere way back in my ancestry—a couple of hundred years or so ago—my great-great-grandfather is reputed to have been an Apache Indian who carried off a rancher's wife before impregnating her,' he dismissed derisively. 'The black hair has appeared in several generations since.'

Dear Lord, this man really was a warrior! Not an axe-wielding, fur-covered Viking, or a kilt-wearing, claymore-brandishing Celt, but a clout-covered, bow-and-arrow-carrying, bareback horse-riding Native American Indian!

It was far too easy for Thia to picture him as such—with that inky-black hair a long waterfall down his back, his muscled and gleaming chest and shoulders bare, just that clout-cloth between him and the horse he rode, the bareness of his long muscled legs gripping—

'Surely I haven't shocked you into silence?' he taunted.

Thia knew by his mocking expression that he wanted her to be shocked, that Lucien Steele was deliberately trying to unnerve her with tales of Apache warriors carrying off innocent women for the sole purpose of ravishing them.

In the same way he was doing the modern

equivalent of carrying her off? Also for ravishment...?

Her chin rose. 'Not in the least.'

Those silver eyes continued to mock her. 'My father is a native New Yorker, but my mother is French—hence I was given the name Lucien. My turn now,' he added softly.

She gave a wary start. 'Your turn to do what...?' she prompted huskily.

Those chiselled lips curled into a derisive smile as he obviously heard the tremble in her voice. 'Ask you a question.'

She moistened dry lips. 'Which is...?'

'Cyn, if you don't stop looking at me like that then I'm going to have to stop the elevator and take you right now.'

As if to back up his statement he pressed a button and halted the lift's descent, before crossing the floor with all the grace of the predator he undoubtedly was and standing just inches in front of her.

Thia's eyes had widened, both at his actions and at the raw desire she could hear beneath the harshness of his tone. 'I—you can't just stop the lift like that…!'

'I believe I already did,' he dismissed arrogantly.

Thia found herself totally unable to look away from the intensity of that glittering silver gaze as Lucien looked down at her from between narrowed lids, her cheeks flushed, her heart beating wildly—apprehensively?—in her chest. 'I—that wasn't a question, either.'

'No.'

She winced. 'How was I looking at you…?'

'As if you'd like to rip my clothes from my body before wrapping your legs about my waist as I push you up against the wall and take you!' His voice was a low and urgent rasp.

Thia's breath caught in her throat as she imagined herself doing any or all of those things, her cheeks flushing, burning. 'I don't think—'

'It's probably better if you don't.'

Lucien Steele's gaze continued to hold hers captive.

She stepped away instinctively, only to feel her back pressing up against the mirrored wall. Lucien Steele dogged her steps until he again stood mere inches away from her and slowly raised his hands to place them on the mirror either side of her head. Lowering his head, he stared down at her with those compelling silver eyes, causing Thia to once again moisten her lips with the tip of her tongue.

'I advise you not to do that again unless you're willing to take the consequences!' he rasped harshly.

Thia's tongue froze on her parted lips as she was once again beset by the feeling of being trapped in the headlights of a car—or, more accurately, the glittering compulsion of Lucien Steele's gaze.

Her throat moved as she swallowed before speaking. 'Consequences?'

He nodded abruptly. 'I'd be more than willing to participate in your fantasy.' His jaw was tight, and desire gleamed in his eyes.

It was a depth of desire Thia had never encountered before, and one that caused her breath to hitch in her throat and her skin to flush with heat: a single-minded depth of desire that made her feel like running for the hills!

'What's Miller to you?' Lucien Steele prompted abruptly.

She blinked long dark lashes. 'Is that your question?'

He bared his teeth in a parody of a smile as he nodded. 'Contrary to my Apache ancestor, I make it a rule never to take another man's woman.'

''Take another man's'—!' She frowned. 'You really *are* something of a barbarian, aren't you?'

Rather than feeling insulted at the accusation, as she had intended, Lucien Steele instead bared his teeth in a wolfish smile. 'You have no idea.'

Oh, yes, Thia definitely had an idea. More than an idea. And her response to this man's raw sexuality terrified the life out of her. Almost as much as it aroused her...

'Cyn?' Lucien pressed forcefully.

She shrugged bare shoulders, those ivory breasts swelling invitingly against her gown. 'I already told you—Jonathan is just a friend—'

'A friend who had no hesitation in hurting you?' Lucien glared his displeasure as he looked down to where dark smudges were already appearing on the smooth paleness of her arm. Her wrist was still slightly red too. 'Who left his mark on you?' he added harshly as he gave in to the temptation to brush his fingertips gently over those darkening smudges.

'Yes...' Her bottom lip trembled, as if she were on the verge of crying. 'I've never seen him behave like that before. He was out of control...' She gave a dazed shake of her head. 'He's never behaved aggressively with me before,' she insisted dully.

'That's something, I suppose.' Lucien nodded abruptly.

'I—would you please restart the lift now...?' Those tears were trembling on the tips of her long dark lashes, threatening to overflow.

He was *scaring* her, damn it!

Because this—his coming on to her so strongly—was too much, too soon after Miller's earlier aggression.

Or just maybe, despite what she might claim to the contrary, her relationship with Miller wasn't as innocent as she claimed it to be...?

In Lucien's experience no woman was as ingenuous as Cyn Hammond appeared to be. Her ingenuousness had encouraged him to reveal more about himself and his family in the last five minutes than he had told anyone for a very long time. Not that Lucien was ashamed of his heritage—it was what it was. It was his private life in general that he preferred to keep exactly that—private.

He straightened abruptly before stepping back. 'A word of advice, Cyn—you should stay well away from Miller in future. He's bad news.'

Her expression sharpened. 'What do you mean?'

'I believe you've more than used up your quota of questions for one evening.' His expression was grim.

'But you seem to know something I don't—'

'I'm sure I know a lot of things you don't, Cyn,' he rasped with finality, before turning to press the button to restart the elevator.

'Thank you,' Cyn breathed softly as it resumed its soundless descent.

'I didn't do it for you.' Lucien gave a hard, dismissive smile. 'The elevator has been stopped between floors for so long now Dex is probably imagining you've assassinated me.'

Thia frowned. 'Is it a defence mechanism, or are you really this arrogant and rude?'

His gaze was hooded as he answered her. 'Quite a bit of the latter and a whole lot of the former.'

'That's what I thought.' She nodded, able to breathe a little easier now that he wasn't standing quite so close to her. Well...perhaps not easier. Lucien Steele's presence was still so overpowering that Thia challenged anyone, man or woman, to be completely relaxed in his company.

He put his hand beneath her elbow again as the lift came to a stop, the doors opening and allowing the two of them to step out into the marble foyer of the luxurious Manhattan apartment building.

Thia's eyes widened as she saw Dex was already there, waiting for them. 'How did you...?'

'Service elevator,' the man supplied tersely, dismissively, his censorious glance fixed on his employer.

'Stop looking so disapproving, Dex,' Lucien Steele drawled. 'I checked before getting in the elevator: there's absolutely nowhere that Miss Hammond could hide a knife or a gun beneath that figure-hugging gown.'

Thia felt the colour warm her cheeks. 'Definitely a *lot* of the latter,' she muttered, in reference to their previous conversation and heard Lucien Steele chuckle huskily beside her even as she turned to give the still frowning Dex a smile. 'Mr Steele does like to have his little joke.'

There was no answering smile from the bodyguard as he opened the door for them to leave. 'I've had the car brought round to the front entrance.'

'Good,' Lucien Steele bit out shortly, his hand still beneath Thia's elbow as he strode towards the black limousine parked beside the pavement, its engine purring softly into life even as Dex moved forward to open the back door for them to get inside.

'I can get a taxi—a cab—from here,' Thia assured Lucien Steele quickly. His behaviour in the lift wasn't conducive to her wanting to get into the back of a limousine with him.

'Get in.'

That compelling expression was back on Lucien Steele's face as he raised one black brow, standing to one side as he waited for her to get into the back of the limousine ahead of him.

Thia gave a pained frown. 'I appreciate your help earlier, but I'd really rather just get a cab from here...'

He didn't speak again, just continued to look down at her compellingly. Because he was so used to everyone doing exactly as he wished them to, whenever he wished it, he had no doubt Thia was going to get into the limousine.

'I could always just pick you up and put you inside...?' Lucien Steele raised dark brows.

'And I could always scream if you tried to do that.'

'You could, yes.' He smiled confidently.

'Or not,' Thia muttered as she saw the inflexibility in his challenging gaze.

Sighing, she finally climbed awkwardly into the back of the limousine. She barely had enough time to slide across the other side of the seat before Lucien Steele got in beside her. Dex closed the door behind them before getting into the front of the car beside the driver and the car moved off smoothly into the steady flow of evening traffic.

'I don't like being ordered about,' Thia informed Lucien tightly.

'No?'

'No!' She glared her irritation across the dim interior of the car. The windows were of smoked glass, as was the partition between the front and back of the car. 'Any more than I suspect you do.' Once again he was intimidating in the close confines of the car, so big and dark, and she could smell his lemon scent again, the insidious musk of the man himself, all mixed together with the expensive smell of the leather interior of the car.

'That would depend on the circumstances and on what I was being ordered to do,' he drawled.

Her irritation deepened along with the blush in her cheeks. 'Do you think you could get your mind out of the bedroom for two minutes?'

He turned, his thigh pressing against hers as he draped his arm along the back of the seat behind her. 'There's no need for a bedroom when this part of the car is completely private and sound-proofed.'

'How convenient for you.'

'For *us*,' he corrected huskily.

Thia's throat moved as she swallowed nervously. 'Unless it's escaped your notice, I'm really not in the mood to play sexual cat-and-mouse games.' She moved her thigh from the warmth of his and edged further along the seat towards the door. 'You offered to drive me home—not seduce me in the back of your car.'

'I believe my original offer was to take you for a quiet drink somewhere,' he reminded her softly.

She gave a shake of her head. 'I'm not in the mood for a drink, either,' she added determinedly.

He smiled slightly in the darkness. 'Then what *are* you in the mood for?'

Thia ignored the innuendo in his voice and instead thought of Jonathan's brutish and insulting behaviour this evening—that reckless glitter in his eyes—all of which told her that it wouldn't be a good idea for her to go back to his apartment tonight. In fact after tonight she believed it would better for both of them if she moved out of Jonathan's apartment altogether and into a hotel, until she flew back to London in a couple of days' time.

Not that she could really afford to do that, but the thought of being any more beholden to Jonathan was no longer an option after the way he had spoken to her earlier. She was also going to repay the cost of the airfare to him as soon as she was able. She was definitely going to have bruises on the top of her arm from where he had gripped her so tightly. It was—

'Cyn?'

She turned sharply to look at Lucien Steele, flicking her tongue out to moisten the dryness of her lips—only to freeze in the action as that glittering silver gaze followed the movement, reminding her all too forcefully of his earlier threat. 'I—could you drop me off at a hotel? An inexpensive one,' she added, very aware of the small amount of money left in her bank account.

This situation would have been funny if Thia hadn't felt quite so much like crying. Here she was, seated in the back of a chauffeur-driven limousine, with reputedly the richest and most powerful man in New York, and she barely had enough money in her bank account to cover next month's rent on her bedsit, let alone an 'inexpensive' hotel!

Lucien Steele pressed the intercom button on the door beside him. 'Steele Heights, please, Paul,' he instructed the driver.

'Will do, Mr Steele,' the disembodied voice came back immediately.

'I totally forgot about the worldwide Steele Hotels earlier in my list of Steele Something-or-Others…' Thia frowned. 'But I'm guessing that none of your hotels are inexpensive…?'

The man beside her gave a tight smile. 'You'll be staying as my guest, obviously.'

'*No!* No…' she repeated, more calmly. 'Thank you. I always make a point of paying my own way.'

Her cheeks paled as she recalled that the one time she hadn't it had been thrown back in her face. She certainly had no intention of being beholden to a man as dangerous as Lucien Steele.

Unfortunately she was barely keeping her head above water now on the money she earned working evening shifts at the restaurant. That would change, she hoped, once she had finished her dissertation in a few months' time and hopefully acquired her Masters degree a couple of months after that. She could then at last go out and get a full-time job relevant to her qualifications. But for the moment she had to watch every penny in order to be able to pay her tuition fees and bills, let alone eat.

A concept she realised the man at her side, with all his millions, couldn't even begin to comprehend…

'Why the smile…?' Lucien prompted curiously.

Cyn gave a shake of her head, that silky dark hair cascading over her shoulders. 'You wouldn't understand.'

'Try me,' he invited harshly, having guessed from her request to go to a hotel that she had indeed been staying at Miller's apartment with him. Lucien had meant it when he'd said he didn't poach another man's woman. *Ever.*

His own parents' marriage had been ripped apart under just those circumstances, with his mother having been seduced away from her husband and son by a much older and even wealthier man than his father. They were divorced now, and had been for almost twenty years, but the acrimony of their separation had taken its toll on Lucien. To a degree that he had complete contempt for any man or woman who intruded on an existing relationship.

The fact that Cyn Hammond claimed she and Jonathan Miller were only friends didn't change the fact that she was obviously staying at the other man's apartment with him. Or at least had been until his aggression this evening...

She gave a grimace as she answered his question. 'I'm a student working as a waitress to support myself through uni. *Now* do you believe you inhabit a different world from me? One where you would think nothing of staying at a prestigious hotel like Steele Heights. I've seen the Steele Hotel in London, and I don't think I could afford to pay the rent on a broom cupboard!'

'I've already stated you will be staying as my guest.'

'And I've refused the offer! Sorry.' She grimaced at her sharpness. 'It's very kind of you,

Lucien, but no. Thank you,' she added less caustically. 'As I said, I pay my own way.'

He looked at her through narrowed lids. 'How old are you?'

'Why do you want to know?' She looked puzzled by the question.

'Humour me.'

She shrugged. 'I'm twenty-three—nearly twenty-four.'

'And your parents aren't helping you through university?'

'I'm sure they would have if they were still alive.' She smiled sadly. 'They were both killed in a car crash when I was seventeen, almost eighteen,' she explained at his questioning look. 'I've been on my own ever since,' she dismissed lightly.

The lightness didn't fool Lucien for a single moment; his own parents had divorced when he was sixteen, so he knew exactly how it felt, how gut-wrenching it was to have the foundations of your life ripped apart at such a sensitive age. And Cyn's loss had been so much more severe than his own. At least his parents were both still alive, even if they were now married to other people.

The things Cyn had told him went a long way to explaining the reason for her earlier smile, though; Lucien had more money than he knew what to do with and Cyn obviously had none at all.

'I can relate to that,' he murmured huskily.

'Sorry?'

'My own parents parted and divorced when I was sixteen. Obviously it isn't quite the same, but the result was just as devastating,' he bit out harshly.

'Is that why you're so driven?'

'Maybe.' Lucien scowled; he really had talked far too much about his personal life to this woman.

'It was tough for me, after the accident, but I've managed okay,' she added brightly. 'Obviously not as okay as you, but even so… I worked for a couple of years to get my basic tuition fees together, so now I just work to pay the bills.'

He frowned. 'There was no money after your parents died?'

Cyn smiled as she shook her head. 'Not a lot, no. We lived in rented accommodation that was far too big for me once I was on my own,' she dismissed without rancour. 'I've almost finished my course now, anyway,' she added briskly. 'And then I can get myself a real job.'

It all sounded like another world to Lucien. 'As what?'

She shrugged her bare shoulders. 'My degree will be in English Literature, so maybe something in teaching or publishing.'

He frowned. 'It so happens that one of those other Steele Something-or-Others is Steele Publishing, with offices in New York, London and Sydney.'

She smiled ruefully. 'I haven't finished my degree yet. Nor would I aim so high as a job at Steele Publishing once I have,' she added with a frown.

Lucien found himself questioning the sincerity of her refusal. It wouldn't be the first time a woman had downplayed the importance of his wealth in order to try and trap him into a relationship.

* * *

Thia had no idea why she had confided in Lucien Steele, of all people, about her parents' death and her financial struggles since then. Maybe as a response to his admission of his own parents' divorce?

She *did* know as she watched the expressions flitting across his for once readable face, noting impatience quickly followed by wariness, that he had obviously drawn his own conclusions—completely wrong ones!—about her reason for having done so!

She turned to look out of the window beside her, stung in spite of herself. 'Just ask your driver to drop me off anywhere here,' she instructed stiffly. 'There are a couple of cheap hotels nearby.'

'I have no intention of dropping you off anywhere!' Lucien Steele rasped. 'This is New York, Cyn,' he added as she turned to protest. 'You can't just walk about the streets at night alone. Especially dressed like that.'

Thia felt the blush in her cheeks as she looked down at her revealing evening gown, acknowledging he was right. She would be leaving herself open to all sorts of trouble if she got out of the car looking like this. 'Then *you* suggest somewhere,' she prompted awkwardly.

'We'll be at Steele Heights in a couple of minutes, at which time I *suggest* you put aside any idea of false pride—'

'There's nothing false about my pride!' Thia turned on him indignantly. 'It's been hard-won, I can assure you.'

'It *is* false pride when you're endangering yourself because of it,' he insisted harshly. 'Now, stop being so damned stubborn and just accept the help being offered to you.'

'No.'

'Don't make me force you, Cyn.'

'I'd like to see you try!' She could feel the heat of her anger in her cheeks.

'Would you?' he challenged softly. 'Is that what all this is about, Cyn? Do you enjoy it…get off on it…when a man bends you to his will, as Miller did earlier?'

'How dare you—?'

'Cyn—'

'My name is *Thia,* damn it!' Her eyes glittered hotly even as she grappled with the door handle beside her, only to find it was locked.

'Tell Paul to stop the car and unlock this damned door. *Now,*' she instructed through gritted teeth.

'There's no need for—'

'Now, Lucien!' Thia breathed deeply in her fury, not sure she had ever been this angry in her life before.

He sighed deeply. 'Aren't you being a little melodramatic?'

'I'm being a *lot* melodramatic,' she correctly hotly. 'But then you were a lot insulting. I don't— Ah, Paul.' She had at last managed to find what she sincerely hoped was the button for the intercom.

'Miss Hammond…?' the driver answered uncertainly.

'I would like you to stop the car right now, Paul, and unlock the back doors, please,' she requested tightly.

There was a brief pause before he responded. 'Mr Steele…?'

Thia looked across at Lucien challengingly, daring him to contradict her request. She was so furious with him and his insulting arrogance she was likely to resort to hitting him if he even attempted to do so.

He looked at her for several more minutes before answering his driver. 'Stop the car as soon as it's convenient, Paul. Miss Hammond has decided to leave us here,' he added, and he turned to look out of the window beside him uninterestedly.

As if she were a petulant child, Thia acknowledged. As if he hadn't just insulted her, accused her of—of— She didn't even want to think about what he had accused her of!

She kept her face turned away from him for the short time it took Paul to find a place to safely park the limousine, her anger turning into heated tears. Tears she had no intention of allowing the cynical and insulting Lucien Steele the satisfaction of seeing fall.

'Thank you,' she muttered stiffly, once the car was parked and Paul had got out to open the door beside her. She kept her face averted as she stepped out onto the pavement before walking away, head held high, without so much as a backward glance.

'Mr Steele...?' Dex prompted beside him uncertainly.

Lucien had uncurled himself from the back of the car to stand on the pavement, his expression grim as he watched Cynthia Hammond stride determinedly along the crowded street in her revealing evening gown, seemingly unaware—or simply uncaring?—of the leering looks being directed at her by the majority of the men and the disapproving ones by the women.

'Go,' Lucien instructed the other man tightly; if Cyn—Thia—had so little concern for her own safety then someone else would have to have it for her.

CHAPTER FOUR

A REALLY UNPLEASANT thing about waking up in a strange hotel room was the initial feeling of panic caused by not knowing exactly where you were. Even more unpleasant was noticing that the less-than-salubrious room still smelt of the previous occupant's body odour and cigarette smoke.

But the worst thing—the *very* worst thing— was returning to that disgusting-smelling hotel bedroom after taking a lukewarm shower in the adjoining uncleaned bathroom and realising that you had no clothes to leave in other than the ankle-length blue evening gown you had worn the night before, along with a pair of minuscule blue panties and four-inch-heeled take-me-to-bed shoes.

All of which became all too apparent to Thia within minutes of her waking up in that awful hotel bedroom and taking that shower!

She had been too angry and upset the evening before—too furious with the arrogantly insulting Lucien Steele—to notice how faded and worn the furniture and décor in this hotel room was, how threadbare and discoloured the towel wrapped about her naked body, let alone the view outside the grimy window of a rusted fire escape and a brick wall.

Thia had been sensible enough the night before, after the lone night porter on duty had openly leered at her when she'd booked in, to at least lock and secure the chain on the flimsy door, plus push a chair under and against the door handle, before crawling between the cold sheets and thin blankets on the bed.

Not that it had helped her to fall asleep—she'd still been too angry at the things Lucien Steele had said to be able to relax enough to sleep.

She dropped down heavily onto the bed now and surveyed what that anger had brought her to. A seedy hotel and a horrible-smelling room that was probably usually let by the hour rather than all night. God, no wonder the night porter had leered at her; he had probably thought she

was a hooker, waiting for her next paying customer to arrive.

At the moment she *felt* like a hooker waiting
for her next paying customer to arrive!

How was she even going to get out of this
awful hotel when she didn't even have any suitable clothes to wear?

Thia tensed sharply as a knock sounded on the
flimsy door, turning to eye it warily. 'Yes…?'

'Miss Hammond?'

She rose slowly, cautiously, to her feet. 'Dex, is
that you…?' she prompted disbelievingly.

'Yes, Miss Hammond.'

How on earth had Lucien Steele's bodyguard
even known where to find her…? More to the
point, *why* had he bothered to find her?

At that moment Thia didn't care how or why
Dex was here. She was just relieved to know he
was standing outside in the hallway. She hurried
across the room to remove the chair from under
the door handle, slide the safety chain across,
before unlocking the door itself and flinging it
open.

'Oh, thank God, Dex!' She launched herself

into his arms as she allowed the tears to fall hotly down her cheeks.

'Er—Miss Hammond...?' he prompted several minutes later, when her tears showed no signs of stopping. His discomfort was obvious in his hesitant tone and the stiffness of his body as he patted her back awkwardly.

Well, of *course* Dex was uncomfortable, Thia acknowledged as she drew herself up straight before backing off self-consciously. What man wouldn't be uncomfortable when a deranged woman launched herself into his arms and started crying? Moreover a deranged woman wearing only a threadbare bathtowel that was barely wide enough to cover her naked breasts and backside!

'I'm so sorry for crying all over you, Dex,' she choked, on the edge of hysterical laughter now, as she started to see the humour of the situation rather than only the embarrassment. 'I was just so relieved to see a familiar face!'

'You—do you think we might go into your room for a moment?' Dex shifted uncomfortably as a man emerged from a room further down the hallway, eyeing Thia's nakedness suggestively as he lingered over locking his door.

'Of course.' Thia felt the blush in her cheeks as she stepped back into the room. 'I—is that my suitcase…?' She looked down at the lime-green suitcase Dex had brought in with him; it was so distinctive in its ugliness that she was sure it must be the same one she had picked up for next to nothing in a sale before coming to New York. The same suitcase that she had intended collecting, along with her clothes, from Jonathan's apartment later this morning… 'How did you get it?' She looked at Dex suspiciously.

He returned that gaze unblinkingly. 'Mr Steele obtained it from Mr Miller's apartment this morning.'

'Mr Steele did…?' Thia repeated stupidly. 'Earlier this morning? But it's only eight-thirty now…'

Dex nodded abruptly. 'It was an early appointment.'

She doubted that Jonathan would have appreciated that, considering he hadn't emerged from his bedroom before twelve o'clock on a single morning since her arrival in New York. 'And Lu—Mr Steele just asked him for my things and Jonathan handed them over?'

Dex's mouth thinned. 'Yes.'

Thia looked at him closely. 'It wasn't quite as simple as that, was it?' she guessed heavily.

He shrugged broad shoulders. 'I believe there may have been a…a certain reluctance on Mr Miller's part to co-operate.'

Thia would just bet there had. Jonathan had been so angry with her yesterday evening that she had been expecting him to refuse to hand over her things when she went to his apartment for them later. An unpleasant confrontation that Lucien Steele had circumvented for her by making that visit himself. She could almost feel sorry for Jonathan as she imagined how that particular meeting would have panned out. Almost. She was still too disgusted with Jonathan's unpleasant behaviour the previous evening to be able to rouse too much sympathy for him.

But she was surprised at Lucien Steele having bothered himself to go to Jonathan's apartment himself to collect her things; Lucien had let her leave easily enough last night, and he didn't give the impression he was a man who would inconvenience himself by chasing after a woman who had walked away from him as Thia had.

She drew a shaky breath. 'No one was hurt, I hope?'

'I wasn't there, so I wouldn't know,' Dex dismissed evenly.

'I had the impression you accompanied Mr Steele everywhere?' Thia frowned her puzzlement.

'Normally I do.' His mouth flattened. 'I spent last night standing guard in the hallway outside this room, Miss Hammond.' He answered her question before she had even asked it.

Thia took a step back in surprise, only to have to clutch at the front of the meagre towel in order to stop it from falling off completely. Her cheeks blushed a furious red as she tried to hold on to her modesty as well as her dignity. 'I—I had no idea you were out there…' Maybe if she had she wouldn't have spent half the night terrified that someone—that dodgy night porter, for one!—

might try to force the flimsy lock on the door and break in.

A suitable punishment, Lucien Steele would no doubt believe, for the way in which she had walked away from him last night! Because there was no way that Dex had spent the night guarding the door to her hotel room without the full knowledge, and instruction of his arrogant employer...

'I doubt you would have been too happy about it if you had.' Dex bared his teeth in a knowing smile before reaching into the breast pocket of his jacket and pulling out an expensive-looking cream vellum envelope with her name scrawled boldly across the front of it. 'Mr Steele had Paul deliver your suitcase here a short time ago, along with this.'

Thia stared at the envelope as if it were a snake about to bite her, knowing that it had to be Lucien Steele's own bold handwriting on the front of it and dreading reading what he had written inside.

At the same time she felt a warmth, a feeling of being protected, just knowing that Lucien had cared enough to ensure her safety last night in spite of herself...

* * *

'A Miss Hammond is downstairs in Reception, asking to see you, Mr Steele. She doesn't have an appointment, of course,' Ben, his PA, continued lightly, 'but she seems quite determined. I wasn't quite sure what I should do about her.'

Lucien looked up to scowl his displeasure at Ben as he stood enquiringly on the other side of the glass-topped desk that dominated this spacious thirtieth-floor office. Lucien wasn't sure himself what to do about Cynthia Hammond.

She was so damned stubborn, as well as ridiculously proud, that Lucien hadn't even been able to guess what her reaction might be to his having had her things delivered to her at that disgustingly downbeat hotel in which she had chosen to stay the night rather than accept his offer of a room at Steele Heights. He certainly hadn't expected that she would actually pay him a visit at his office in Steele Tower.

And he should have done—Cynthia Hammond was nothing if not predictably unpredictable. 'How determined is she, Ben?' He sighed

wearily, already far too familiar with Cyn's stubbornness.

'Very.' His PA's mouth twitched, as if he were
holding back a smile.

The wisest thing to do—the *safest* thing to do
for Lucien's own peace of mind, which would be
best served by never seeing the beautiful Cynthia
Hammond again—would be to instruct Security
to show her the door…as if she didn't already
know exactly where it was! But if Cyn was determined enough to see him, then Lucien didn't
doubt that she'd just sit there and wait until it was
time for him to leave at the end of the day.

He pulled back the cuff on his shirt and glanced
at the plain gold watch on his wrist. 'I don't leave
for my next appointment for ten minutes, right?'

'Correct, Mr Steele.'

He nodded abruptly. 'Have Security show her
up.'

Lucien leant back in his high-backed white
leather chair as Ben left the office, knowing this
was probably a mistake. He already knew, on just
their few minutes' acquaintance the evening before, that Cynthia Hammond was trouble.

Enough to have caused him a night full of dreams of caressing that pearly skin, of making love to her in every position possible—so much so that he had woken this morning with an arousal that had refused to go down until he'd stood under the spray of an ice-cold shower!

He had even had Paul drive by the hotel where he knew she had spent the night on his way to visit Jonathan Miller's apartment this morning. The neighbourhood was bad enough—full of drug addicts and hookers—but the hotel itself was beyond description, and fully explained Dex's concern when he had telephoned Lucien the night before to tell him exactly which hotel Cyn had checked into and to ask what he should do about it. What the hell had possessed her to stay in such a disreputable hovel?

Money. Lucien answered his own question. He knew from his conversation earlier that morning with Jonathan Miller that Cyn really was exactly what she had said she was: a student working as a waitress to put herself through university, and just over here for a week's visit.

Her finances were not Lucien's problem, of

course, but he had been infuriated all over again just looking at the outside of that disgusting hotel earlier, imagining that vulnerable loveliness protected only by the flimsy door Dex had described to him. Dex had been so worried about the situation Lucien believed the other man would have decided to stand guard over her for the night whether Lucien had instructed him to do so or not!

Just another example of the trouble Cynthia Hammond caused with her—

'*Wow!* This is a beautiful building, Lucien! And this office is just incredible!'

Lucien also gave a *wow,* but inwardly, as he glanced across the room to where Cynthia Hammond had just breezily entered his office. A Cynthia Hammond whose black hair was once again a straight curtain swaying silkily to just below her shoulders. The beautiful delicacy of her face appeared free of make-up apart from a coral-coloured lipgloss and the glow of those electric blue eyes. She was dressed in a violent pink cropped sleeveless top that left her shoulders and arms bare and revealed at least six inches of her bare and slender midriff—as well as the fact that she wore no bra beneath it. And below that bare midriff was the tightest pair of skinny low-rider blue denims Lucien had ever seen in his life. So tight that he wondered whether Cyn wore any underwear beneath...

And that was just the front view. Ben's admiring glance, as he lingered in the doorway long enough to watch Cyn stroll across the spacious office, was evidence that the back view was just as sexily enticing!

Cyn did casual elegance well—so much so that Lucien felt decidedly overdressed in his perfectly tailored black suit, navy blue silk shirt and black silk tie. 'Don't you have some work to do, Ben?' he prompted harshly as he stood up—and then sat down again as he realised his arousal had sprung back to instant and eager attention. The benefits of his icy cold shower earlier this morning obviously had no effect when once again faced with the enticing Cynthia Hammond.

Trouble with a capital T!

'Thanks, Ben.' Thia turned to smile at the PA before he closed the door on his way out, then returned her gaze to the impressive office rather than the man seated behind the desk, putting off the moment when she would have to face the disturbing Lucien Steele. Just a brief glance in his direction as she had entered the cavernous office had been enough for her to feel as if all the air had been sucked from her lungs, and her nerve-endings were all tingling on high alert.

This black and chrome office was not only beautiful, it was *huge*. Carpeted completely in black, it had an area set aside for two white leather sofas and a bar serving coffee as well as alcohol, and another area with a glass and marble conference table, as well as Lucien Steele's own huge desk, bookshelves lining the wall behind him, and an outer wall completely in glass, giving a panoramic view of the New York skyline.

It really was the biggest office Thia had ever seen, but even so her gaze was drawn as if by a magnet inevitably back to the man seated behind the chrome and black marble desk. The office was easily big enough to accommodate half a dozen executive offices, and yet somehow— by sheer force of will, Thia suspected—Lucien

Steele still managed to dominate, to *possess*, all the space around him.

As he did Thia?

Maybe she should have power-dressed for this meeting rather than deciding to go casual? She did have one slim black skirt and a white blouse with her—they would certainly have blended in with the stark black, white and chrome décor of his office. Much more so than her shockingly pink cropped top.

Oh, well, it was too late to worry about that now. She would have to work with what she had.

'Say what you have to say, Cyn, and then go,' Lucien Steele bit out coldly. 'I have to leave for another appointment in five minutes.'

Her breath caught in her throat as she looked at Lucien. A Lucien who was just as knee-tremblingly gorgeous this morning as the previous night. Thia had convinced herself during her restless night of half-sleep that no one could possibly be that magnetically handsome, that she must have drunk too much of the Carews' champagne and imagined all that leashed sexual power.

She had been wrong. Lucien Steele was even

more overpoweringly attractive in the clear light of day, with the sun shining in through the floor-to-ceiling windows turning his hair that amazing blue-black, his bronzed face dominated by those silver eyes, and his features so hard and chiselled an artist would weep over his male beauty. And as for the width of those muscled shoulders—!

Time for her to stop drooling! 'Nice to see that you're still living up to my previous description of you as being arrogant and rude,' she greeted with saccharine sweetness.

He continued to look at her coldly with those steel-grey eyes. 'I doubt you want to hear my opinion of *you* after the stunt you pulled last night.'

She felt the colour warm her cheeks and knew he had to be referring to the hotel in which she had spent the night, which Dex would no doubt have described to his employer in graphic detail. 'I didn't have the funds to stay anywhere else.'

'You wouldn't have needed any funds if you had just accepted the room I offered you at Steele Towers,' Lucien reminded her harshly.

'Accepting the room you offered me at Steele

Towers would have put me under obligation to you,' she came back, just as forcefully.

Lucien stilled, eyes narrowing to steely slits. 'Are you telling me,' he asked softly, 'that the reason you refused my offer last night was because you believed I would expect to share that bedroom with you for the night as payment?'

'Well, you can't blame me for thinking that after the way you came on to me outside on the balcony and then again in the lift!'

Lucien raised dark brows. 'I can't *blame* you for thinking that?'

'Well…no…' Cyn eyed him, obviously slightly nervous of his quiet tone and the calmness of his expression.

And she was wise to be! Because inwardly Lucien was seething, furious—more furious than he remembered being for a very long time, if ever. Even during the visit he had paid to Jonathan Miller's apartment earlier this morning he had remained totally in control—coldly and dangerously so. But just a few minutes spent in the infuriating Cynthia Hammond's company and Lucien was ready to put his hands about her throat and throttle her!

If it weren't for the fact that he knew he would much rather put his hands on another part of her anatomy, starting with that tantalisingly bare and silky midriff, and stroke her instead...

Thia took a step back as Lucien Steele stood up and moved round to the front of his desk. His proximity, and the flat canvas shoes she was wearing, meant she had to tilt her head back in order to be able to look him in the face. A face that made her wish she were an artist. What joy, what satisfaction, to commit those hard and mesmerising features to canvas. Especially if Lucien could be persuaded into posing in traditional Apache clout cloth, with oil rubbed into the bare bronzed skin of his chest and arms, emphasising all the dips and hollows of those sleek muscles—

'What are you thinking about, Cyn?'

She looked up guiltily as she realised her appreciative gaze had actually wandered down to that muscled chest as she imagined him bare from the waist up—. 'I—you—nice suit.' She gave him a falsely bright smile.

Lucien Steele's mouth tilted sceptically, as if he knew exactly what she had been thinking. 'Thanks,' he drawled derisively. 'But I believe we were discussing your reckless behaviour last night and your reasons for it?' His voice hardened and all humour left his expression. 'Do you have any idea what could have happened to you if Dex hadn't stayed outside your room all night?'

She had a pretty good idea, yes. 'It was stupid of me. I accept that.'

'Do you?' he bit out harshly.

She nodded. 'That's why I'm here, actually. I wanted to thank you.' She grimaced. 'For allowing Dex to stand guard last night. For having my things delivered to the hotel this morning. And for sending that keycard, in the envelope Dex gave me, for a suite at Steele Heights.'

For all her expectations of what Lucien Steele *might* have put in that vellum envelope Dex had handed her this morning, there had been nothing in it but a keycard for a suite at Steele Heights, which he had obviously booked for her.

Thia had wrestled with her pride over accepting, of course, along with that old adage about accepting sweets from strangers. This was a different sort of suite, of course, but she told herself it was still sensible to be wary. But pride and wariness weren't going to put a roof over her head tonight, and she couldn't possibly go back to Jonathan's.

Lucien leant back against his desk and seemed to guess some of her thoughts. 'I trust you've overcome your scruples and moved in there now?'

'Yes.' Thia grimaced. Just the thought of that luxurious suite—the sitting room, bedroom and equally beautiful adjoining bathroom—was enough for her to know she had done the right thing. It might take her a while, but she fully intended to reimburse Lucien for his generosity.

He quirked one dark brow. 'Does that mean you no longer mind feeling under obligation to me?'

Thia looked up at him sharply, unable to read anything from his mocking expression. 'I think the question should be do *you* believe I'm under any obligation to you?'

'Let me see...' He crossed his elegantly clad legs at the ankles as he studied her consideringly. 'I left a perfectly good party last night because I thought we were going on somewhere to have a drink together. A drink that never happened. You flounced off in a snit after I offered to drive you somewhere, which greatly inconvenienced me as Dex was then forced to stand guard over your room all night. And I was put to the trouble this morning of asking your ex-boyfriend to pack up your belongings in that hideous lime-green suitcase before having my driver deliver it to that seedy hotel.' He gave a glance at the slender gold watch on his wrist. 'Your unexpected visit here this morning means I am now already three minutes late leaving for my next appointment. So what do *you* think, Cyn? *Are* you obligated to me?'

Well, when he put it like that... 'Maybe,' Thia allowed with a pained wince.

'I would say there's no *maybe* about it.' He slowly straightened to his full height of several inches over six feet, that silver gaze fixed on her unblinkingly as he took a step forward.

Thia took a step back as she was once again overwhelmed by the unique lemon and musk scent of Lucien Steele. 'What are you doing?'

'What does it look as if I'm doing?'

He was standing so close now she could feel the warmth he exuded from his body against the bareness of her midriff and arms. His face— mouth—only was inches away from her own as he lowered his head slightly.

She moistened her lips with the tip of her tongue. 'It looks to me as if you're trying to in- timidate me!'

He gave a slow and mocking smile as he re- garded her through narrowed lids. 'Am I suc- ceeding?'

'You must know that you intimidate everyone.'

'I'm not interested in everyone, Cyn, just you.'

Thia's heart was beating such a loud tattoo in her chest that she thought Lucien must be able to hear it. Or at least see the way her breasts were quickly rising and falling as she tried to drag air into her starved lungs. 'You're standing far too close to me,' she protested weakly.

He tilted his head, bringing those chiselled lips even closer to hers. 'I like standing close to you.'

She realised she liked standing close to Lucien too. That she liked him. That she wanted to do so much more than stand close to him. She wanted Lucien to pull her into his arms and kiss her. To make love to her.

Which was strange when she had never felt the least inclination to make love with any man before now. But Lucien wasn't just any man. He was dark and dangerous and overpoweringly, mesmerisingly, sexually attractive—a combination Thia had never come across before now. She knew her breasts had swelled, the nipples hard nubs, pressing against her cropped top, and between her thighs she was damp, aching. For Lucien Steele's touch!

As if he was able to read that hunger in her face, Lucien's pupils dilated and his head slowly lowered, until those beautiful sculptured lips laid gentle but hungry siege to hers.

Thia felt as if she had been jolted with several thousand volts of electricity. And heat. Such burning heat coursing through her. She stepped in closer to that hard, unyielding body and her arms moved up and over Lucien's wide shoulders as if of their own volition. The warmth of his strong hands spanned the slenderness of her bare waist as her fingers became entangled in that silky black hair at his nape, her lips parting as she lost herself in the heat of his kiss.

Trouble…

Oh, yes, Cyn Hammond, with her black hair, electric-blue eyes, beautiful face and deliciously enticing body, was definitely Trouble with a capital T…

But at this moment, with the softness of her responsive lips parted beneath his, his hands caressing, enjoying the feel of the soft perfection of her bare midriff, Lucien didn't give a damn about that.

Nothing had changed since last night. If anything he wanted her more than he had then.

Again. Right here.

And right now!

Lucien deepened the kiss even as he moulded her slender curves against his own much harder ones, intoxicated, lost in Cyn's taste as he ran his tongue along the pouting softness of her bottom lip. Groaning low in his throat, he let his tongue caress past those addictive lips and into the heat beneath, plunging, possessing that heat as his hands moved restlessly, caressingly, down the length of her spine. Soon Lucien was able to cup that shapely bottom and pull her snugly into and against the pulsing length of his arousal.

The softness of her thighs felt so good against his, so hot and welcoming. He shifted, the hardness of his shaft now cupped and cushioned in that softness, and moved one of his hands to cup her breast through her T-shirt. It was a perfect fit into the palm of his hand, the nipple hard as an unripe berry as Lucien brushed the soft pad of his thumb across it and heard Cyn's gasp of pleasure, felt her back arching, pressing her breast harder into his cupping hand in a silent plea.

Her skin felt as smooth as silk beneath Lucien's fingertips as he slipped his hand beneath the bottom of her top to cup her bare breast—

Thia wrenched her mouth from Lucien's and pulled out of his arms before taking a stumbling step backwards—as if those few inches in any way nullified Lucien's sexual potency, or the devastation wrought upon her senses by that hungry kiss and those caressing hands!

'No…' she breathed shakily, her cheeks ablaze with embarrassed colour as she attempted to straighten her top over breasts that pulsed and ached for the pleasure she had just denied them.

Lucien's gaze was hooded. There was a flush across those high cheekbones, a nerve pulsing in his clenched jaw. 'No?'

'No,' Thia repeated more firmly. 'This is—I don't do this.'

'"This" being…?'

'Seduction in a zillionaire's office!'

He arched one dark brow. 'How many zillionaires do you know?'

Her cheeks warmed. 'Just the one.'

He nodded. 'That's what I thought.' He crossed his arms in front of his chest and he looked at her from between narrowed lids. 'Just what did you think was going to happen, Cyn, when you came to my office dressed—or rather undressed—like that?' That glittering silver gaze swept appreciatively over her breasts, naked beneath the crop top, her bare midriff and hip-hugging denims.

She hadn't allowed herself to think before coming here—had just acted on impulse, knowing she had to thank Lucien Steele for his help some time today and just wanting to get it over with. But, yes, now that he mentioned it she wasn't exactly dressed for repelling advances. Deliberately if subconsciously so? Lord, she hoped not!

'Stop calling me Cyn,' she snapped defensively.

'But that's what you are to me... Sin and all that word implies.' He all but purred. 'You have all the temptation of a candy bar in that shocking pink top. One that I want to lick all over.'

Thia felt heat in her already blushing cheeks at the provocative imagines that statement conjured in her mind. 'You—I don't—didn't—' She gave a shake of her head. 'Could we get back to our earlier conversation?' *Please,* she added silently, knowing she would have plenty of time later today to think about and to remember with embarrassment the touch of Lucien's lips and hands on her body. 'For one thing, Jonathan was only ever my friend,' she continued determinedly.

'Not any more he isn't.' Lucien nodded with grim satisfaction. 'He made it clear before I left his apartment earlier this morning that he was feeling decidedly less than charitable towards you,' he explained dryly.

Thia's eyes widened. 'What did you say to him?'

'About you?' He shrugged. 'As you have neither a father nor brother to protect you, I thought it necessary that someone should warn Miller against laying so much as a finger on you with the intention of hurting you ever again.'

She gasped. 'I can look after myself!'

'Is that why you spent the night at a less-than-reputable hotel? Why you have bruises on your arm?' Lucien's expression darkened with displeasure as his glittering silver gaze moved to the purple-black smudges at the top of her left arm. 'If I had known the extent of your bruising I would have inflicted a few of my own on him this morning, rather than just firing his ass!'

Thia gasped even as she looked up searchingly into that ruthlessly handsome face, totally unnerved by the dangerous glitter in Lucien's eyes as he continued to glower at the bruises on her arms. 'You fired Jonathan from *Network?*'

He looked up into her face as he gave a humourless smile of satisfaction. 'Oh, yes.'

Oh, good grief...

CHAPTER FIVE

LUCIEN'S HUMOURLESS SMILE became a grimace as he saw the expression of horror on Cyn's face. 'Don't worry. My decision to fire Miller wasn't because of anything he did or said to you. Although that was certainly a side issue in the amount of satisfaction I felt doing it.'

'Then why did you fire him?' She looked totally bewildered.

Lucien gave another impatient glance at his wristwatch. 'Look, can we continue this conversation later? Possibly over dinner? I really do have to leave for my appointment now.' He moved around his desk to pick up the file he needed for his meeting before putting it inside his black leather briefcase and snapping it shut. 'Cyn?' he prompted irritably as she stood as still as an Easter Island statue.

He was more than a little irritated with himself

for having suggested the two of them have dinner together when he knew that the best thing for both of them was not be alone together again. His response to Cyn—as he had proved a short time ago!—was so different than to any other woman he had ever met. She was so different from those preening, self-centred, high-maintenance women he usually dated...

'Hmm?' She looked across at him blankly.

'Dinner? Tonight?' he repeated shortly.

'I—no.' She shook her head from side to side. 'You've been very kind to me, but—'

'You consider my almost making love to you just now as being *kind* to you...?' Lucien bit out derisively.

Her cheeks flushed a fiery red. 'No, of course not—'

'Dinner. Tonight,' he said impatiently. He couldn't remember the last time he had been late for a business appointment. Business always came first with him, pleasure second. And making love to Cyn just now had been pure pleasure. 'We can eat at the hotel if that would make you feel...*safer?*' he taunted.

* * *

Thia easily heard the mockery in Lucien's voice. A mockery she knew she deserved.

So Lucien had kissed her. More than kissed her. She wasn't a child, for goodness' sake, but a twenty-three-year-old woman, and just because this was the first time that anything like this had happened to her it was no reason for her to go off at the deep end as if she were some scandalised Victorian heroine!

Besides which, it was obvious Lucien wasn't going to tell her any more now about why he had fired Jonathan, and she desperately wanted to know.

Was it even possible for him to dismiss Jonathan so arbitrarily? Admittedly this was Lucien Steele she was talking about—a man who had already proved how much he liked having his own way—but surely Jonathan had a contract that would safeguard him from something like this happening. Besides which, *Network* was the most popular series being shown on US television at the moment; sacking its English star would be nothing short of suicide for both the series *and* Steele Media. And Lucien *was* Steele Media.

'Fine, we'll eat at Steele Heights,' she bit out abruptly. 'What time and which restaurant?' There were three of them, but obviously Cyn hadn't eaten at any.

Lucien moved briskly from behind his desk, briefcase in hand, and took hold of her elbow with the other hand. 'We can talk about that in the car before I drop you off at the hotel.'

'I'm not going back to the hotel just yet.' Thia dug her heels in at being managed again, even as she recognised that familiar tingling warmth where Lucien's fingers now lightly touched her arm. 'I'm going to the Empire State Building this afternoon.'

He raised dark brows. 'Why?'

'What do you mean, *why?*' She looked up at him irritably. 'It's a famous New York landmark, and I've been here five days already and not managed to go to the top of it yet.'

Lucien's mouth twisted derisively. 'I was born in New York, have lived here most of my thirty-five years, and I can honestly say I've never been even to the top of the Empire State Building.'

'You could always come with me—' Thia broke off as she realised the ridiculousness of her suggestion. Of course Lucien Steele, zillionaire entrepreneur, didn't want to do something as mundane as go with her to the top of the Empire State Building any more than Thia really wanted him to accompany her. Did she…? No, of course she didn't. She had succumbed to this man's sexual magnetism enough for one day—made a fool of herself enough for one day—thank you very much.

'Forget it,' she dismissed, with a lightness she was far from feeling. She wasn't one hundred per cent sure *what* she was feeling at the moment, or thinking. She was too tremblingly aware of Lucien having kissed her just minutes ago to be able to put two coherent thoughts together. 'You said you had a meeting to get to?' she reminded him.

Yes, he did. But strangely, just for a few seconds, Lucien had actually been considering cancelling his business meeting and going with Cyn to visit the Empire State building instead. Unbelievable.

Zillionaires didn't get to be or stay zillionaires, by playing hooky from work to go off and play tourist with a visitor from England. Even if—*especially* if—that visitor was Cyn Hammond. A woman who apparently had the ability to make Lucien forget everything but his desire to be with her and make love to her.

Something that had definitely not happened to him before today.

But, damn it, Cyn really did look like a tempting stick of candy in that pink top… And it took no effort at all on Lucien's part to imagine the pleasure of licking his tongue over every inch of that soft and silky flesh…

He nodded abruptly. 'I can drop you off at the Empire State Building on my way.'

'It's such a lovely day I think I'd rather walk,' she refused lightly, lifting a hand in parting to Ben as they passed through his office and out into the hallway before stepping into the private elevator together.

Just the thought of Cyn wandering the streets

of New York dressed in nothing more than that skimpy pink top and those body-hugging denims was enough to bring a dark scowl back to Lucien's brow. 'Do you have *any* sense of self-preservation at all?' he rasped harshly as he released her elbow to press the button for the elevator to take them down to the ground floor.

'It's the middle of the day, for goodness' sake!' She glanced at him with those cobalt blue eyes through lushly dark lashes.

Lucien eyed her impatiently. 'Remind me to tell you later tonight about the statistics for daytime muggings and shootings in New York.'

She chewed on her bottom lip. 'You still have to tell me what time I'm meeting you this evening, and at which restaurant in the hotel,' she said firmly.

'Eight o'clock.' He frowned. 'Go down to the ground floor. I'll have someone waiting to show you to the private elevator that will bring you directly up to the penthouse apartment.'

Her eyes widened. 'The penthouse? You live in an apartment at the top of the Steele Heights

Hotel?' Thia was too surprised not to gape at him incredulously.

He gave a smile of satisfaction at her reaction. 'I occupy the whole of the fiftieth floor of Steele Heights when I'm in New York.'

'The whole floor?' she gasped. 'What do you have up there? A tennis court?'

'Not quite.' Lucien smiled tightly. 'There is a full-sized gym, though. A small pool and a sauna. And a games room. A small private cinema for twenty people.' He quirked a dark brow as Cyn gaped at him. 'Changed your mind about having dinner with me at the hotel this evening?' Those silver eyes mocked her.

It didn't take too much effort on Thia's part to realise Lucien was challenging her, daring her. He expected her to baulk at agreeing to have dinner with him now that she knew they would be completely alone in his penthouse apartment. And good sense told Thia that it would be a wise move on her part *not* to rise to this particular challenge, to just withdraw and concede Lucien as being the winner.

Unfortunately Thia had never backed down

from a challenge in her life. She wouldn't have been able to survive the death of her parents or worked as a waitress for the past five years in order to support herself through uni if that was the case. And she had no intention of backing down now, either.

Even if she did suspect that Lucien wasn't just challenging her by inviting her to his apartment and that the main reason he wanted them to dine in the privacy of his apartment was because he didn't want to be seen out with her in public.

She knew enough about Lucien Steele to know he was a man the media loved to photograph, invariably entering some famous restaurant or club, and always with a beautiful model or actress on his arm. Being seen with a waitress student from London hardly fitted in with that image.

'Fine.' She nodded abruptly. 'Eight o'clock. Your apartment.'

'No need to dress formally,' Lucien told her dismissively. 'Although perhaps something a little less revealing than what you're currently wearing might be more appropriate,' he added dryly.

'It's a crop top, Lucien. All women are wearing them nowadays.'

'None of the women *I've* escorted have ever done so,' he assured her decisively.

'That's your loss!' Thia felt stung by Lucien's casual mention of those women he'd escorted. Which was ridiculous of her. The fact that they were eating dinner at his apartment told her that this wasn't a date, just a convenient way for the two of them to be able to finish their conversation in private. Well away from the public eye...

'Yes.' He bared his teeth in a wolfish smile as the two of them stepped out of the lift together, causing Thia to blush as he reached out to grasp one of her hands lightly in his before raising it to skim his lips across her knuckles. 'Until later, Cyn.'

Thia snatched her hand from within his grasp, aware of the stares being directed their way by the other people milling about in the lobby of Steele Tower even if he wasn't. 'I hope you're enjoying yourself,' she hissed, even as she did her best to ignore the tingling sensation now coursing the length of her arm. And beyond...

'It has its moments.' His eyes glittered with satisfied amusement as he looked down at her.

Thia glared right back at him. 'You could have told me your reason for firing Jonathan in the time we've been talking together.'

'I do things my own way in my own time, Cyn,' he bit out tersely. 'If you have a problem with that, then I suggest—'

'I didn't say I had a problem with it,' she snapped irritably. 'Only that—oh, never mind!' Lucien had the ability to rob her of her good sense, along with any possibility of withstanding his lethal attraction.

A lethal attraction that affected every other woman in his vicinity, if the adoring glances of the receptionists were any indication, as well as those of the power-dressed businesswomen going in and out of the building.

All of them, without exception, had swept a contemptuous gaze over the casually dressed Thia—no doubt wondering what a man like Lucien Steele was doing even wasting his time talking to someone like her—before returning that gaze longingly, invitingly, to the man at Thia's side. One poor woman had almost walked into a potted plant because she had been so preoccupied with eating Lucien up with her eyes!

It was a longing Thia knew she was also guilty of.

Challenge or no challenge, she really shouldn't have agreed to have dinner alone with him in his apartment this evening...

Thia looked in dismay at the chaos that was her bedroom in the suite on the tenth floor of the Steele Heights Hotel. Clothes were strewn all over the bed after she had hastily tried them on and then as quickly discarded them. Finding exactly the right casual outfit to wear to have dinner with the dangerously seductive Lucien Steele in—oh, hell—fifteen minutes' time was proving much more difficult than she had thought it would. And she hadn't dried her hair yet, or applied any make-up.

She had been late getting back to the hotel as the long queues at the Empire State Building had meant she'd had to wait in line for a long time before getting to the top. It had been worth the wait when she finally got there, of course, but by that time it had been starting to get late.

She'd also had the strangest feeling all afternoon that she was being followed...

Lucien's warnings earlier had made her paranoid. That was more than a possibility. Whatever the reason, Thia had felt so uncomfortable by the time she'd come down from the top of the Empire State Building and stepped back out into the street that she had decided to treat herself and take a taxi back to the hotel.

She had taken out her laptop and gone online for half an hour once she was back in the hotel suite, determined to know at least a little more about the enigmatic Lucien Steele before they met again this evening.

Unfortunately the moment she'd come offline and lain back on the bed she had fallen asleep, tired from her outing, and also exhausted from the previous sleepless night she had spent at that awful hotel. No surprise, then, that she hadn't woken up again until almost seven-thirty!

Which now meant she was seriously in danger of being late—and she still hadn't found anything to wear that she thought suitable for having dinner with a man like Lucien Steele!

Oh, to hell with it. Black denims and a fitted blouse the same colour blue as her eyes would have to do; she simply didn't have any more time to waste angsting over what she should or shouldn't wear to have dinner with a zillionaire. And the blue blouse also had the benefit of having elbow-length sleeves, meaning those bruises Jonathan had inflicted on her arm the previous evening, which had so angered Lucien earlier, would be safely hidden from his piercing gaze.

Jonathan....

If she concentrated on the fact that it was only because she wanted to know exactly why Lucien had decided to fire Jonathan from *Network* that she had agreed to have dinner with Lucien—even if she no longer believed that!—then maybe she would be able to get through this evening.

The butterflies fluttering about in her stomach didn't seem to be listening to her assurances as she stood alone in the private lift minutes later, on her way up to the penthouse apartment. Her hair still wasn't completely dry and her face felt flushed. No doubt it looked it too, despite her application of a light foundation.

The manager of the hotel himself had been waiting on the ground floor to show her into the private coded lift. The sheer opulence of the lift in which she was now whizzing up fifty floors to the penthouse apartment—black carpet, plush bench seat along one mirrored wall, a couple of pot plants—and the thought of the overwhelmingly sexy man who would be waiting up there for her were so far beyond what was normal for Thia, was it any wonder she was so nervous she felt nauseous?

Or maybe it was just the thought of being alone with Lucien again that was making her feel that way... Her online snooping about him earlier had informed her that he was thirty-five years old—something Lucien had already told her—and the only child of New Yorker Howard Steele and Parisian Francine Maynard. Educated at private school and then Harvard, he had attained a law degree and in his spare time designed a new gaming console and graphics for many computer games, enabling him to make his first million—

or possibly billion?—before he was twenty-one. That was something else Lucien had already told her. He had taken full advantage of this success by diversifying those millions into any number of other successful businesses.

There had also, depressingly, been dozens of photographs of him with dozens of the women he had escorted at some time or other during the past fifteen years: socialites, actresses, models. All of them, without exception, were extremely beautiful, as well as being tall and blond.

And this was the man that Thia, five-foot-two, raven-haired and merely pretty, had agreed to have dinner alone with this evening...

Knowing she simply wasn't his type should have made her feel less nervous about the evening ahead. Should have. But it didn't. How could it when she only had to think of the way Lucien had kissed her so intensely this afternoon, of his caressing hands on her bare midriff—and higher!—to know that he had felt desire for her then, even if she *was* five-foot-two and raven-haired!

After all her apprehension, the man who had

caused all those butterflies in her stomach was nowhere to be seen when Thia stepped out of the lift into the penthouse apartment seconds later. The apartment itself was everything she had thought it would be—white marble floors, original artwork displayed on ivory walls. She walked tentatively down the hallway to the sitting room in search of Lucien. It was a spaciously elegant room, with the same minimalist white, black and chrome décor of Lucien's office. Had the man never heard of any other colours but white, black and chrome?

The view from the floor-to-ceiling windows was even more spectacular than the one from the Carews' apartment—

'I'm sorry I wasn't here to greet you when you arrived, Cyn. My meeting ran much later than I had anticipated and I only got back a few minutes ago.'

Thia turned almost guiltily at the sound of Lucien's voice, very aware of the fact that she had just walked into his private apartment and made herself at home, only to stand and stare, her mouth falling open, blue eyes wide and unblinking, as she took in his rakishly disheveled and practically nude appearance.

Lucien had obviously just taken a shower. His black hair was still damp and tousled, a towel was draped about his shoulders, and he wore only a pair of faded blue denims sitting low down on the leanness of his hips, leaving that glistening bronzed chest and shoulders—the same ones Thia had fantasised about earlier this afternoon!—openly on view. Revealing he was just as deliciously muscled as she had imagined he would be. His nipples were the size and colour of two dark bronze coins amongst the dusting of dark hair that dipped and then disappeared beneath the waistband of his denims.

If Lucien had wanted to lick her all over this afternoon then Thia now wanted to do the same to him... Dressed in those low-slung denims, with his bronzed shoulders and chest bare, overlong blue-black hair sexily dishevelled, his bare feet long and elegant, Lucien definitely looked good enough to eat!

'Cyn...?' Lucien eyed her questioningly as she made no response.

Or perhaps she did…

She was wearing another pair of those snug-fitting denims this evening—black this time—with a fitted blouse the same electric blue colour as her sooty-lashed eyes. The material of the blouse was so sheer it was possible for Lucien to see that she wore no bra beneath it. Her breasts were a pert shadow, nipples plump as berries as they pressed against the soft gauzy material. Hard and aroused berries…

'I—er—shouldn't you go and finish dressing…?'

Lucien dragged his gaze slowly, reluctantly away from admiring those plump, nipple-crested breasts to look up into Cyn's face, instantly noting the flush to her cheeks and the almost fevered glitter to her eyes as she shifted uncomfortably from one booted foot to the other. As if her breasts weren't the only part of her body that was swollen with arousal…

Instead of doing as she suggested Lucien stepped further into the sitting room. 'I'll get you a drink first.' He threw the damp towel down onto a chair as he strolled over to the bar in the corner of the room. 'Bottled water, white wine, red wine...something stronger...?' He arched a questioning brow.

Was Lucien strutting his bare, bronzed stuff deliberately? Thia wondered. As a way of disconcerting her? If he was then he was succeeding. She had never felt so uncomfortably aware of a man in her life as she was now by all his warm naked flesh. Or so aroused!

The man should have a public health warning stamped on his chest. Something along the lines of 'Danger to all women with a pulse' ought to do it. And Thia was the only woman with a pulse presently in Lucien Steele's disturbing vicinity! Her throat felt as if it had closed up completely, and her chest was so tight she could barely breathe, let alone speak.

She cleared her throat before even attempting it. 'Red wine would be lovely, thank you,' she finally managed to squeak, in a voice that sounded absolutely nothing like her own, only to draw a hissing breath into her starved lungs as Lucien turned away from her. The muscles shifted in his back beneath that smooth bronzed skin as he bent to take a bottle of wine from the rack beside the bar, and even more muscles flexed in his arms as he straightened to open it, the twin dips at the base of his spine clearly visible above the low-riding denims.

Twin dips Thia longed to stroke her tongue over, to taste, before working her way slowly up the length of that deliciously muscled back...!

'Here you go.' Lucien strolled unconcernedly across the room carrying two glasses of red wine—one obviously meant for Thia, the other for himself.

Evidence that he didn't have any intention of putting any more clothes on in the immediate future? And why should he? This was his home, after all!

His close proximity now meant that Thia was instantly overwhelmed by that smell of lemons and the musky male scent she now associated only with this man, and her hand was trembling slightly as she reached out to take one of the wine glasses from him—only to spill some of the wine over the top of the glass as a jolt of electricity shot up her arm the moment her fingers came into contact with his.

'Sorry,' she mumbled self-consciously, passing the glass quickly into her other hand with the intention of licking the spilt wine dripping from her fingers.

'Let me…' Lucien reached out to catch her hand in his before it reached her parted lips, his gaze easily holding hers as he carried her fingers to his own mouth before lapping up the wine with a slow and deliberate rasp of his tongue. 'Mmm, delicious.' He licked his lips. 'Perhaps I should consider always drinking wine this way…?' His shaft certainly thought it was a good idea as it rose up hard and demanding inside his denims!

'Lucien—'

'Hmm?' He continued to lick the slenderness of Cyn's silky fingers even after all the wine had gone, enjoying the way her hand was trembling in his and watching the slow rise and fall of those plumped breasts and aroused nipples, his erection now almost painful in its intensity.

She snatched her hand away from his to glare up at him. 'Are you doing this on purpose?'

'Doing what…?'

Her eyes narrowed. 'Would you please go and put some clothes on?'

Lucien straightened slowly to look at her from between narrowed lids. 'You seem a little…tense this evening, Cyn. Didn't the Empire State live up to your expectations?'

'The Empire State was every bit as wonderful as I always imagined it would be. And I'm not in the least tense!' She moved away jerkily until she stood apart from him.

Far enough that she thought she had put a safe distance between them.

Lucien was so aroused right now he didn't think the other side of the world would be far enough away to keep Cyn safe from him…

His meeting that afternoon had not gone well. No, that wasn't accurate. It hadn't been the meeting that was responsible for his feelings of impatience and dissatisfaction all afternoon. That had been due to the intrusive thoughts he'd had of Cyn all through that lengthy meeting—not just the silkiness of her skin, her responsive breasts, the delicious taste of her mouth, but also the fact that he *liked* her…her sense of humour, the way she answered him back, everything about her, damn it! It had caused Lucien to finally call a halt to negotiations and reschedule the meeting for another day next week.

Needless to say he had not been best pleased that he had allowed the distraction of those thoughts of Cyn to infringe on his business meeting, but one look at her tonight, dressed in those snug-fitting black denims and the delicate blue blouse, with the silky darkness of her hair loose about her shoulders, and his earlier feeling of irritated dissatisfaction had instantly been replaced by desire.

'I thought that I had been invited up here for dinner,' she snapped now. 'Not to witness a male strip show!'

Lucien made no effort to hold back his grin of satisfaction at her obvious discomfort at seeing his bare chest. It seemed only fair when he had thought of her all afternoon. When his shaft was now an uncomfortable, painful throb against his denims. 'I'm wearing more now than I would be on a beach,' he reasoned.

'Unless you haven't noticed, we don't happen to *be* on a beach.' She frowned. 'And I do not have any intention of providing your amusement for the evening.'

He eyed her mockingly. 'Oh, I haven't even begun to be amused yet, Cyn.'

'And as far as I'm concerned you aren't going to be, either!' She placed her glass down noisily on the coffee table before straightening and turning, with the obvious intention of walking out on him.

Lucien reached out and grasped her arm as she would have stormed past him—only to ease up on the pressure of that grasp as he saw the way she winced. 'Are your wrist and arm still hurting you?' he rasped.

'No. I—they're fine.' She gave a dismissive shake of her head, her eyes avoiding meeting his piercingly questioning gaze. 'You just caught me unawares, that's all.'

'I don't believe you.'

She sighed her impatience. 'I don't care whether or not— What are you doing?' she demanded as Lucien released her arm before moving his hands to the front of her blouse, his fingers unfastening the tiny blue buttons. 'Lucien? Stop it!' She slapped ineffectually at his hands.

'I don't trust your version of "fine", Cyn. I intend to see for myself,' Lucien muttered grimly as he continued unfastening those buttons.

'Stop it, I said!' She pulled sharply away from him—a move immediately followed by a delicate ripping sound as Lucien refused to release his hold. The gauzy blouse ripped completely away from the last remaining buttons, leaving Cyn's breasts completely bared to his heated gaze.

Full and beautifully sloping breasts...tipped by two perfect rosy-red nipples...those nipples were plumping and hardening in tempting arousal as Lucien continued to look down at them appreciatively.

CHAPTER SIX

'I CAN'T BELIEVE you just did that!' Thia was the first to recover enough to speak, staring accusingly at Lucien even as her shaking hands scrabbled desperately to pull the two sides of her blouse together over her bared breasts, feeling mortified by her nakedness in front of a man she already found far too overpoweringly attractive for comfort.

Her knees had once again turned to the consistency of jelly at the heat she saw in those silver eyes…!

'I believe, if you think about it, you'll find that *we* just did that,' Lucien drawled hardly. 'You pulled away. I didn't let go.' He shrugged.

Thia bristled indignantly, clutching on to anger as a means of hiding her embarrassment—and arousal—at the continued heat in Lucien's gaze.

'You shouldn't have been unbuttoning my blouse in the first place!'

'I wanted to see your bruises. I still want to see them,' he added determinedly.

'You saw a lot more than my bruises!' she snapped. 'And I believe we've already had one discussion about my feelings concerning what you do or don't want. In this instance what you wanted resulted in the ruination of a blouse I was rather fond of and saved for weeks to buy.'

'I'll replace it for you tomorrow.'

'Oh, won't that be just wonderful?' She huffed her exasperation. 'I can hear your telephone conversation with the woman in the shop now—*Send a blue blouse round to Miss Hammond's suite at Steele Heights Hotel. I ripped the last one off her!*' She attempted to mimic his deep tones. 'Are you laughing at me, Lucien?' Thia eyed him suspiciously and she thought—was *sure!*—she saw his lips twitch.

He chuckled softly. 'Admiring the way you sounded so much like me.'

'Well, I certainly can't stay and have dinner with you *now.*'

'Why not?' All amusement fled and his expression darkened.

'Hello?' She gave him a pitying look. 'Ripped blouse and no bra?'

'I noticed that.' Lucien nodded, silver eyes once again gleaming with laughter even if his expression remained hard and unyielding. 'We've met three times now, and on none of those occasions have you been wearing a bra,' he added curiously.

Thia's cheeks blushed a fiery red as she thought of the revealing gown she had been wearing last night—no way could she have been wearing a bra beneath *that*. And the intimacy of Lucien's caresses in his office earlier today had shown him that she hadn't been wearing a bra under her pink crop top, either. As for ripping her blouse just now and baring her breasts…!

'I—the uniform I have to wear when I'm working at the restaurant is of some heavy material that makes me really hot, so I usually go without one and it's just become a habit,' she explained defensively.

'Don't get me wrong. I'm not complaining.'

'Why am I not surprised?' If she were honest,

Thia's initial shock and anger were already fading and she now felt a little like laughing herself—slightly hysterically—at this farcical situation. Hearing her blouse rip, seeing the initial shock on Lucien's face, had been like something out of a sitcom. Except Thia didn't intend letting him off the hook quite that easily…

Oh, she had no doubt that ripping her blouse had been an accident, and that she was as much to blame for it as Lucien was. But if he hadn't been behaving quite so badly by insisting on having his own way—again!—he would never have been in a position to rip her blouse in the first place. Or to bare her breasts. And that really had been embarrassing rather than funny.

Besides, she really did find Lucien far too disturbing when he was only wearing a pair of faded denims and showing lots of bare, muscled flesh. Her ripped blouse was the perfect excuse for her to cry off having dinner with him this evening.

'We haven't talked about the Jonathan Miller situation yet.'

Lucien had just—deliberately?—said the one thing guaranteed to ensure Thia stayed exactly where she was!

* * *

Lucien had found himself scowling at the idea of Thia working in a public restaurant night after night, wearing no bra, with those delicious breasts jiggling beneath her uniform for all her male customers to see and ogle.

Just as it now displeased him that Cyn was so obviously rethinking her decision about not having dinner with him only because he had mentioned the Jonathan Miller situation.

The other man had physically hurt her, was responsible for her having had nowhere to sleep last night other than that disreputable hotel, and yet Miller hadn't given a damn what had happened to her when he'd thrown her belongings haphazardly into a suitcase this morning and handed them over to Lucien.

Worst of all, Lucien now knew, from his conversation with Miller, that the other man had been using Cyn for his own purposes. He had believed—wrongly, as it happened—that her presence in his apartment in New York would give the impression that his affair with Simone

Carew, was over. Something Cyn was still totally unaware of...

'Well?' he rasped harshly.

She gave a pained frown. 'Perhaps you have a T-shirt I could wear? And maybe you could find one for yourself while you're at it?' she added hopefully.

How did this woman manage to deflate his temper, to make him want to smile, when just seconds ago he had been in a less than agreeable mood at how distracted he had been all afternoon? Because of this woman...

But smile he did as he crossed his arms in front of his chest. 'It really bothers you, doesn't it?'

'All that naked manly chest stuff? Yes, it does.' She nodded. 'And it isn't polite, either.'

'That was a rebuke worthy of my mother!' Lucien was no longer just smiling. He was chuckling softly.

'And?'

'And far be it from me to disobey any woman who can scold like my mother!'

'You're so funny.' She eyed him irritably.

He gave an unconcerned shrug. 'I'll get you one

of my T-shirts.' No doubt Cyn would look sexy as hell in one of his over-large tops!

Her eyes narrowed suspiciously. 'You're being very obliging all of a sudden.'

Lucien quirked a dark brow. 'As opposed to...?'

'As opposed to your usual bossy and domineering self—' She broke off to eye Lucien warily as he dropped his arms back to his sides before stepping closer to her.

'You know, Cyn,' he murmured softly, 'it really isn't a good idea to insult your dinner host.'

'Would that be the same dinner host who almost ripped my blouse off me a few minutes ago?'

The very same dinner host who would enjoy nothing more than ripping the rest of that blouse from her body! The realisation made Lucien scowl again.

This woman—too young for him in years and experience, and far too outspoken for her own good—made him forget all his own rules about the women in his life—namely, only older, experienced women, who knew exactly what they were getting—or rather what they were not going to get from him, such as marriage and for ever—when they entered into a relationship with him.

He'd had little time even for the *idea* of marriage after his parents had separated and then divorced so acrimoniously, and making his own fortune before he was even twenty-one had quickly opened his eyes to the fact that most women saw only dollar signs when they looked at him, not the man behind those billions of dollars.

So far in their acquaintance Cyn Hammond had resisted all his offers of help, financial or otherwise, and that pride and independence just made him like her more.

'Good point.' He straightened abruptly. 'I'll be back in a few minutes.'

Thia admired Lucien's loose-limbed walk as he left the room, only able to breathe again once she knew she was alone. She knew from that determined glitter in Lucien's eyes just now that she had only barely—literally!—managed to avert a possibly physically explosive situation. Just as she knew she wasn't sure if she had the strength of will to resist another one...

The truth was her breasts tingled and she grew damp between her thighs every time she so much as dared a glance at all that fascinating naked and bronzed flesh!

Lucien was without doubt the most nerve-sizzling and gorgeous man Thia had ever seen. His whole body was muscled and toned but not too much so, in that muscle-bound and unattractive way some men were. And as for the strength and beauty of that perfectly chiselled face...!

All that wealth and power, and the man also had a face and body that would make poets of both sexes wax lyrical. Hell, *she* was writing a sonnet in her head about him!

And now she was completely alone with him, in his fiftieth floor apartment, with her tattered and ripped blouse pulled tightly across her bare breasts...

She should have kept to her earlier decision to leave. Should have made her escape as quickly and as—

'Here you go—what is it?' Lucien questioned

sharply, having come back into the room and seen how pale Cyn's face had become in his absence. Her eyes were dark and troubled smudges between those sooty lashes. 'Cyn?' he prompted again concernedly as she only continued to look at him nervously, with eyes so dark they appeared navy blue.

Her creamy throat moved as she swallowed before speaking. 'I think it would be better if I left now, after all…'

Lucien frowned. 'What have you eaten today?'

She looked puzzled by the change of subject. 'No breakfast, but I bought a hot-dog from a street vendor on the way to the Empire State Building for lunch.'

'Then you need to eat. Put this T-shirt on and then we'll go into the kitchen and see what Dex has provided us with to cook for dinner.' He held out the white T-shirt he had brought back for her to wear, having pulled on a black short-sleeved polo shirt over his own naked chest. A naked chest that had seemed to bother her as much as she bothered him…

Her eyes widened. 'Does Dex do your food shopping for you, too?'

'When necessary, yes.'

'What else does he do for you…?'

'Many, many things,' Lucien drawled derisively.

'You probably wouldn't know how to go about buying your own groceries anyway,' she dismissed ruefully.

'Probably not,' he acknowledged easily. 'Does it bother you that we're eating here?'

Cyn shrugged. 'I just assumed you would be ordering hotel room service this evening.'

'Most of the time I do.' He nodded.

'But you decided tonight would be an exception?' she said knowingly.

'I just thought you would prefer to eat here. Don't tell me.' He grimaced. 'You don't know how to cook?'

'Of course I know how to—' She broke off, eyes narrowing suspiciously. 'You're challenging me to get your own way again, aren't you?'

He quirked a brow. 'Is it working?'

Some of the tension eased from her expression. 'Yes.'

He nodded. 'Then that's exactly what I'm doing.'

Cyn eyed him frustratedly. 'Why are you so determined to keep me here?'

Lucien had absolutely no idea! Especially when he had initially made the suggestion of dinner in his apartment just to see what Cyn's reaction would be. Boy, had *that* backfired on him! 'Why are you so determined to leave?' he came back challengingly.

'Yep, the face of an angel and the wiles of the devil...'

Lucien heard her mutter the words irritably. 'Sorry?' he said. He knew exactly what Cyn had said—he just wanted to see if he could get her to say it again. Especially the part where she said he had the face of an angel...

'Nothing.' Cyn refused to humour him and gave a rueful shake of her head. 'Okay, give me the T-shirt.' She took it out of his outstretched hand before holding it up defensively in front of her breasts. 'Why don't you just disappear off into the kitchen while I slip off my blouse and put this on?' she prompted as he made no effort to leave.

'And if I'd rather stay here and watch you slip off your blouse...'

He enjoyed the flush that instantly coloured her cheeks. Enjoyed teasing Cyn, full-stop. So much so that, despite her being so disruptive and stubborn, teasing her was fast becoming one of Lucien's favourite pastimes. Exclusively so.

'Life is just full of little disappointments!' she came back, with insincere sweetness.

'Oh, it wouldn't be a *little* disappointment, Cyn,' he assured her huskily. And it wouldn't be; Lucien could imagine nothing he would enjoy more than to see Cyn strip out of her blouse, allowing him to look his fill of those pert little breasts and plump, rose-coloured nipples.

'Go,' she instructed firmly.

'And you accuse *me* of being bossy...'

'You've made a fine art of it. I'm just doing it out of self-defence.'

Lucien gave a wicked 'wiles of the devil' grin. 'Do you need defending from me?'

She eyed him irritably. 'Now you're deliberately twisting my words.'

He shrugged. 'Maybe that's because you're trying to spoil my fun.'

She gasped. 'Because I won't let you stand there and gawp at me while I change my blouse?'

'I never *gawp,* Cyn,' he drawled derisively. 'If I stayed I would just stand here quietly and appreciate.'

Her face warmed. 'You aren't staying.'

Lucien gave another appreciative grin; she really was cute when she got her dander up.

Cute? He had never found a woman *cute* in his life!

Until now...

Because Cyn, all hot and bothered and clutching his T-shirt tightly to her as if it were her only defence, was most definitely cute.

'Okay, I'll leave you to change,' he murmured dryly. 'I'll take the bottle of wine and glasses through with me.'

'Fine.' She nodded distractedly.

Anything to get him out of the room while she changed her top, Lucien acknowledged ruefully as he collected up the bottle of wine and glasses before leaving. As if such a flimsy barrier—*any* barrier!—could have stopped him if he had decided he wanted her naked!

'Did you have Dex follow me today...?' Thia prompted huskily when she entered the kitchen.

Lucien turned from taking food out of the huge chrome refrigerator that took up half the space of one wall in what was a beautiful kitchen—white marble floors again, extensive kitchen units a pale grey, a black wooden work table in the middle of the vast room, silver cooking utensils hanging from a rack next to a grey and white cooker. No doubt there was a dishwasher built into one of those cabinets, too.

He hadn't answered her question yet...

'Lucien?' she said softly as she lifted her replenished glass from the table and took a sip of red wine.

'I got so distracted by how sexy you look in my T-shirt that I've forgotten what the question was,' he came back dryly.

No, he hadn't. This man didn't forget anything.

Ever. And his prevarication was answer enough. He *had* instructed Dex to follow her this afternoon. And Thia wasn't sure how she felt about that. Annoyed that he had dared to have her followed at all, but also concerned as to why he continued to feel it necessary…

And sexy was the last thing she looked in Lucien's white T-shirt. The shoulder seams hung halfway down her arms, meaning that the short sleeves finished below her elbows, and it was so wide across the chest it hung on her like a sack, so long it reached almost to her knees. Well… it didn't hang *completely* like a sack. Thia realised as she glanced down. Colour once again warmed her cheeks as she saw the way the T-shirt skimmed across the tips of her breasts. Across the hard, aroused thrust of her nipples!

Even so, *ridiculous* was the word Thia would have used to describe her current appearance, not sexy.

'*Did* you have Dex follow me today?' she repeated determinedly.

'I did, yes.'

'Can I ask why?' she prompted warily.

'You can if you can make salad and ask at the same time.' Lucien seemed totally relaxed as he placed the makings of a salad down on the kitchen table before returning to the fridge for steaks.

Thia rolled her eyes. 'I'm a woman, Lucien. Multi-tasking is what we do best.' She took the salad vegetables out of the bags and put them in the sink to wash them.

'That sounds…interesting.' He turned to arch mocked brows.

She was utterly charmed by this man when he became temptingly playful. And she shouldn't allow herself to be.

It wasn't just those twelve years in age that separated them, it was what Lucien had done in those twelve years that set them so far apart—as evidenced by all those photographs of him on-line, taken with the multitude of women he had briefly shared his life with. Or, more accurately, his bed.

And at the grand age of twenty-three Thia was still a virgin. Not deliberately. Not even consciously as in 'saving herself' for the man she loved and wanted to marry.

She had just been too busy keeping her life together since her parents died to do more than accept the occasional date, and very rarely a second from the same man. Jonathan had been the exception, but even he had become just a friend rather than a boyfriend. Thia had never been even slightly tempted to deepen their relationship into something more.

And yet in the twenty-four hours she had known Lucien Steele she seemed to have thought of nothing else but how it would feel to go to bed with him. To make love with him.

Weird.

Dangerous!

Because Lucien might desire her, but he didn't do falling in love and long-term relationships. And why should he when he could have any woman—as many women as he wanted? Except...

'What are you thinking about so deeply that it's making you frown...?' he asked huskily.

Thia snapped herself out of imagining how it

would feel to have Lucien Steele fall in love with her. A ridiculous thought when she so obviously wasn't his type.

And yet here she was, in this apartment, with a relaxed and charming Lucien, and the two of them intended to cook dinner together just like any other couple spending the evening at home together.

She took another sip of wine before answering him. 'Nothing of any importance,' she dismissed brightly as she put the wine glass down to drain the vegetables. 'Do you have any dressing to go with the salad or shall I make some?'

'Can you do that?'

Thia gave him a scathing glance as she crossed the room to open the vast refrigerator and look inside for ingredients for a dressing. 'I'm a waitress, remember?'

'You're a student, working as a waitress in your spare time,' he corrected lightly.

She straightened slowly. 'No, I'm actually a waitress who's working for a degree in my spare time,' she insisted firmly. 'And you still haven't answered my original question.'

'Which was…?'

'Why did you have Dex follow me today?' she repeated determinedly, knowing that Lucien was once again trying to avoid answering one of her questions.

He shrugged. 'Dex suggested it was necessary. I agreed with him.'

'What does that mean?'

'It means that he was obviously as concerned about your walking about New York on your own as I was. You might have been robbed or attacked. Speaking of which…' Lucien strolled across the kitchen, checking her wrist first, which was only slightly reddened from where Jonathan's fingers had twisted it, before gently peeling back the sleeve of the white T-shirt. He drew in a hissing breath as he saw the livid black and blue bruises on the top of her arm.

'They look worse than they feel.' Thia pulled out of his grasp before turning to take down a chopping board and starting to dice vegetables for the salad. 'Isn't it time you started cooking the steaks…?' she prompted dryly.

'Deflection is only a delaying tactic, Cyn.

Sooner or later we're going to talk about those bruises,' he assured her grimly.

'Then let's make it later,' she dismissed. 'Steaks, Lucien?' she repeated pointedly when she turned to find him still watching her from between narrowed lids.

He gave a deep sigh. 'Okay, Cyn, we'll do this your way for now,' he conceded. 'We'll eat first and then we'll talk.'

'It really is true what they say—men don't multi-task!' She smiled teasingly.

'Maybe we just prefer to do one thing at a time and ensure that we do it really, really well?' Lucien murmured huskily, suggestively, and made a determined effort to damp down the renewed anger he felt at seeing those bruises on Cyn's delicately lovely skin.

Colour washed over her cheeks. 'You're obviously wasting your talents as an entrepreneur, Lucien; you should have been a comedian.'

But what Lucien was actually doing was mirroring her own deflection...

Because he was once again so angry after seeing Cyn's bruises—bruises inflicted by Miller—

that he didn't want to have to answer her question as to why he'd had Dex follow her on her outing this afternoon just yet.

Oh, he accepted that he would have to answer it some time—just not yet. Talking about the reason Dex had followed her to the Empire State Building earlier, and how his concern was directly linked to Jonathan Miller, was not conducive to the two of them being able to enjoy cooking and eating a meal together. And, despite Lucien's earlier irritation, he was totally enjoying Cyn's company.

'How do you like your steak?' he prompted as he moved to turn up the heat beneath the griddle, hoping he remembered how to cook steaks. Cyn's assumption earlier had been a correct one: it had been years since Lucien had cooked for himself or anyone else.

'Medium rare, please,' she answered distractedly as she put the salad into a wooden bowl. 'Are we eating in here or in the dining room?'

'Which would you prefer?'

Her brows rose. 'You're actually asking for my opinion about something now?'

Lucien turned to lean back against one of the kitchen cabinets. 'Smart-mouthed young ladies are likely to get their bottoms spanked!'

Her eyes widened. 'Dinner hosts who threaten their female guests are likely to get cayenne pepper sprinkled on their half of the salad dressing. What is it?' she questioned curiously as Lucien began to chuckle. 'You aren't used to being teased like this, are you?' she realised slowly.

'No, I'm not,' he conceded ruefully, unable to remember the last time anyone had dared to tease him, let alone argue with him in the way that Cyn so often did. 'My mother does it occasionally, just to keep it real, but only mom/son stuff.' He shrugged.

Cyn eyed him wistfully. 'Have you remained close to both your parents?'

He nodded. 'I don't see either of them as often as I could or should—but, yeah, I've stayed close to both of them.'

'That's nice.'

Lucien looked at her searchingly. 'Don't you have any family of your own?'

'None close, no.' She grimaced. 'Don't feel

sorry for me, Lucien,' she added lightly as he still frowned. 'I had great parents. I lost them a little earlier than I would have wished or wanted, but I still count myself lucky to have had them to love and be loved by for seventeen years.'

The more Lucien came to know about Cynthia Hammond, the more he came to appreciate that she really was unlike any other woman he had ever known. So obviously beautiful—inside as well as out. And that outward beauty she could so easily have used to her advantage these past six years, if she had wanted to, by snaring herself a rich husband to support her. Instead she had chosen independence.

No feeling sorry for herself at the premature death of her parents. She was just grateful to have had them for as long as she had. And instead of bitching about the necessity to fend for herself after their deaths she had picked herself up and started working her way through university. And instead of bemoaning the fact that Jonathan Miller, a man she had believed to be her friend, had let her down royally since she'd come to New York she had done all she could to remain loyal to him.

It was fast becoming an irresistible combination to Lucien when coupled with the fact that she was so bright and bubbly she made him laugh, was mouthwateringly beautiful, and obviously intelligent.

She also, Lucien discovered a short time later—once the two of them were seated opposite each other at the small candlelit table in the window of the dining room, where they could look out over the city—ate with such passionate relish that he found himself enjoying watching her, devouring her with his eyes rather than eating his own food.

The expression of pleasure on her face as she took her first forkful of dessert—a New York cheesecake from a famous deli in the city—was almost orgasmic. Her eyes were closed, cheeks flushed, pouting lips slightly moist as she licked her tongue across them.

Lucien groaned inwardly as his erection, having remained painfully hard and throbbing inside his denims during the whole of dinner, rose even higher, seeming to take on a life of its own. To such a degree that he had to shift on his seat in order to make himself more comfortable!

Not that he was complaining. No, not at all. His thoughts had turned to the possibility of taking Cyn to his bed, of making love to her until he saw that same look on her face over and over again as he pleasured her to orgasm after orgasm.

'That was…indescribably good.' Thia sighed her pleasure as she placed her fork down on her empty dessert plate. 'Aren't you going to eat yours…?' She hadn't realised until now that Lucien was watching her rather than eating his own cheesecake.

Dinner with Lucien Steele had been far more enjoyable than she had thought it would be. The food had been good, and the conversation even more so as they'd discussed their eclectic tastes in books, films, television and art. Surprisingly, their opinions on a lot of those subjects had been the same, and the times when they hadn't been they had argued teasingly rather than forcefully. Thia liked this more relaxed Lucien. Too much so!

Lucien pushed his untouched dessert plate across the table towards her. 'You have it.'

'I couldn't eat another bite,' Thia refused, before chuckling huskily. 'I bet you're doubly glad now not to be seen out in public with me. I've realised since I've been here that it isn't really the done thing in New York for a woman to actually *enjoy* eating. We're supposed to just pick at the food on our plate before pushing it away uninterestedly. I've always enjoyed my food too much to be able to do that.' She gave a rueful shake of her head. 'Besides, it's rude not to eat when someone has taken you out for a meal or cooked for you. And I've enjoyed this much more than going out, anyway. Cooking dinner is probably the first normal thing I've done since coming to New York! Do you think…?' Her voice trailed off as she realised that Lucien had gone very quiet.

An unusual occurrence for him, when he seemed to have something to say on so many other subjects!

'Lucien…?' Thia eyed him warily as she saw the way his eyes glittered across at her with that intense silver light. His mouth had thinned, his jaw tensed—all signs, she recognised, of his displeasure.

What had she said to annoy him? Perhaps he hadn't liked her comment on the expectations of New York society? After all, he was a member of that society.

Whatever she had said, Lucien obviously wasn't happy about it...

CHAPTER SEVEN

THERE WAS A cold weight of anger in Lucien's chest, making it difficult for him to breathe, let alone speak. Cyn actually thought—she believed that he—

Lucien stood up abruptly, noisily, from the table, thrusting his hands into his pockets as he turned to look sightlessly out of the window, breathing deeply through his nose in an effort to control that anger. If he said anything now he was only going to make the situation worse than it already was.

'Lucien?'

The uncertainty, hesitation in Cyn's voice succeeded in annoying him all over again. Just minutes ago they had been talking so comfortably together—occasionally arguing light-heartedly about a book, a film or a painting they had both read or seen, but for the most part finding they shared a lot of the same likes and dislikes.

That easy conversation, coupled with Cyn's obvious enjoyment of the food they had prepared, had resulted in Lucien feeling relaxed in her company in a way he never had with any other woman. Not completely relaxed. He was too aware of everything about her for that: her silky midnight hair, those beautiful glowing cobalt blue eyes, her flushed cheeks, the moist pout of her lips, the way his borrowed T-shirt hugged the delicious uptilting curve of her breasts whenever she moved her arms to emphasise a point in conversation... But Cyn's complete lack of awareness of Lucien's appreciation of those things had been another part of his enjoyment of the evening. There had been none of the overt flirting that he experienced with so many other women, or the flaunting of her sexuality in an effort to impress him. Cyn had just been her usual outspoken self. An outspoken self that he found totally enticing...

And now this!

He drew a deep breath into his starved lungs

before turning back to face her, his own face slightly in shadow as he stood out of the full glow of the flickering candlelight. 'You believe I made a conscious decision not to take you out to a restaurant for dinner this evening because I didn't want to be seen publicly in your company?'

Ah. That was the comment that had annoyed him...

Thia gave a dismissive shrug. 'It's no big deal, Lucien. Believe me, I've seen photos of the women you usually escort, and I don't even come close—'

'Seen how?' he prompted suspiciously.

She gave a self-conscious grimace. 'I—er— checked you out online earlier this evening,' she admitted reluctantly, wishing Lucien wasn't standing in the shadows so that she could see the expression on his face.

'Why did you do that?'

'Because I wanted to know more about the man I had agreed to have dinner with, alone in his apartment,' she came back defensively. 'I was using that sense of self-preservation you seem to think I have so little of.'

He gave a terse inclination of his head. 'And after reading about me online, seeing photographs of the women I usually escort, you came to the conclusion I was deliberately keeping you hidden away in my apartment this evening because I didn't want to be seen out in public with you?'

'Oh, no. I decided that after you made the invitation earlier today,' Thia dismissed easily.

His brows rose. 'Can I ask why?'

She sighed heavily. 'When was the last time you cooked dinner for a woman in your apartment?'

'What does that—?'

'Just answer the question, please, Lucien,' she cajoled teasingly.

He shrugged. 'I think tonight is the first time I've cooked dinner in my apartment at all—let alone for or with a woman.'

'Exactly.' Thia had noticed earlier that none of the state-of-the-art equipment in the kitchen looked as if it had ever been used.

His mouth thinned. 'If you must know, I made the invitation initially because I suspected your having dinner alone with me here would throw you into something of a panic, and I wanted to see what you would do.'

'And I called your bluff and accepted.' She gave a rueful shake of her head.

'Yes, you did.' He nodded slowly.

'Probably best not to challenge me again, hmm?'

'I don't regret a single moment of this evening.' Thia's cheeks bloomed with heated colour as she recalled the earlier part of the evening, when Lucien had ripped her blouse. 'You were also aware, because I told you so last night, that New York society has absolutely no interest in furthering its acquaintance with a waitress from London. Just think how shocked they would have been to see Lucien Steele in a restaurant with *me!*'

He breathed his impatience. 'I don't give a damn what anyone else thinks.'

'I'm really not in the least offended by any of this, Lucien.' Thia smiled. 'I had a good time this evening. As for New York society…I don't enjoy their company either, so why should it bother me what any of them think of me?'

'Do you have so little interest in what *I* might think of you?' he prompted softly.

That was a difficult question to answer. Thia was so attracted to Lucien that of course it mattered to her whether or not he liked her—just as it mattered what he thought of her. But by the same token it also didn't. Because they wouldn't ever see each other again after tonight. Even the money for the suite, which Thia was so determined to pay back to him, no matter how long it took her to do so, could be sent to his office at Steele Tower when the time came. They had no reason to see each other again once she left here this evening. Which, although disappointing, was just a fact of life. Their totally different lives…

'I like to think I'm a realist, Lucien,' she answered lightly. 'Zillionaire Lucien Steele—' she pointed to him '—and Cynthia Hammond, waitress/student, living from payday to payday.' She pointed to her own chest. 'Not exactly a basis for friendship.'

'I have no interest in being your *friend!*' he rasped with harsh dismissal.

She flinched at the starkness of his statement. 'I believe I just said that—'

'I have no interest in being your friend because I want to be your lover. Touch me.' Lucien stepped forward to grasp her hand impatiently in his before lifting it to the bulge at the front of his denims.

Evidence of an arousal that Thia had been completely unaware of until that moment. She couldn't possibly remain unaware of it now—not when she could feel the long, hard length of Lucien's swollen shaft, the heat of it burning her fingertips as she stroked them tentatively against him. Her eyes widened as she felt the jolt, the throb, of that arousal in response to her slightest caress.

She moistened her lips with the tip of her tongue and looked up at Lucien. 'Does one preclude the other...?'

His mouth twisted derisively. 'In my experience, yes.'

In Thia's limited experience too...

She'd only dated maybe half a dozen times these past six years, and had always ended up being friends with those men rather than lovers. Including Jonathan. Although she suspected that their friendship had ceased after his behaviour yesterday, and yet again this morning, when he had packed her belongings into her suitcase and handed it over to Lucien seemingly without a second thought as to where or how she was.

'Stop thinking about Miller,' Lucien rasped.

She blinked. 'How did you know—?'

'I think I'm intelligent enough to know when the woman I'm with is thinking about another man,' he bit out harshly, having known from the way Cyn's gaze had become slightly unfocused that her attention was no longer completely here with him. Which, considering her hand was currently pressed against his pulsing erection, was less than flattering.

She gave a rueful smile. 'I sincerely doubt it's happened to you often enough for that to be true.'

'It's never happened to me before, as far as I'm aware,' he grated.

He lifted her hand away impatiently before

pulling her to her feet, so that she now stood just inches in front of him. His other hand moved beneath her chin to raise her face, so that she had no choice but to look up at him. 'And, yes, I was challenging you earlier. I wanted to unnerve you a little by inviting you to my apartment. But I did *not* have dinner with you here as a way of hiding you away. I'm insulted that you should ever have thought that I did.' He was more than insulted— he actually felt hurt that Cyn could believe him capable of behaving in that way where she was concerned...

Thia could see that he was. His eyes glittered dangerously, there was angry colour along those high cheekbones, his lips had thinned and his jaw thrust forward forcefully.

'I apologise if I was mistaken.'

'You were,' he bit out. 'You still are.'

She nodded; Lucien was too upset not to be telling her the truth.

'Have I succeeded in ruining the evening?' She looked up at him through long dark lashes.

Lucien eyed her impatiently. 'I have absolutely no idea.'

She drew in a shaky breath. 'How about we clear away in here while you decide?'

His eyes narrowed. 'Are you humouring me, Thia?'

The fact that Lucien had called her Thia for the first time was indicative of how upset he was. 'Is it working?' she deliberately used the same phrase he had to her earlier, when she had challenged him about always wanting his own way.

Some of the tension left his shoulders. 'Maybe a little,' he conceded dryly. 'And we can just blow out the candles in here and leave all this for housekeeping to clear away in the morning.' He indicated the dinner table beside them.

Thia's stomach did a somersault. 'Oh...'

He gave a rueful shake of his head. 'I have no idea how you do that...'

'Do what?' She looked up at him curiously.

'Make me want to laugh when just seconds ago I was so angry with you I wanted to kiss you senseless!' He gave a self-disgusted shake of his head as the last of his earlier tension eased from his expression.

'Senseless, hmm?' Thia eyed him teasingly. 'According to you, that wouldn't be too difficult!'

'See?' Lucien chuckled wryly, shaking his head.

The sudden hunger in Lucien's gaze told Thia this was the ideal time for her to suggest she return to her own suite in the hotel, to thank Lucien for dinner, and his company and conversation, and then leave, never to see or hear from him again.

It was the latter part of that plan that stopped her from doing any of those things… 'Does one preclude the other?' she repeated provocatively, daringly.

'You *want* me to kiss you senseless…?' he prompted gruffly.

She drew in a sharp breath, knowing this was a moment of truth. 'Even more than I enjoy watching you laugh,' she acknowledged shyly.

Lucien's piercing gaze narrowed on her searchingly. 'Be very sure about this, Thia,' he finally warned her. 'I want you so badly that once I have you in my bed I'm unlikely to let you out of it again until I've made love to you at least half a dozen times.'

Thia's heart leapt as he jumped from kissing her senseless to taking her to his bed. Her heart pounded loudly in her chest at the thought of all that currently leashed but promised passion. Of having this man—having *Lucien Steele!*—want to make love to her with such an intensity of feeling. It was an intensity of passion she didn't know, in her inexperience, that she could even begin to match...

But she would at least like to the opportunity to try!

'Can you do that? I thought that men needed to...to rest for a while...recuperate before...well, you know...'

He arched dark brows. 'Let's give it a try, shall we? Besides, I don't recall giving any time limit for making love to you those half a dozen times.'

No, he hadn't, had he? Thia acknowledged even as her cheeks burned. In embarrassment or excitement? She really wasn't sure! 'I only have one more full day left before I leave New York, and don't you have to go to work tomorrow?'

'Not if I have you in my bed, no,' Lucien assured her softly.

Thia's heart was now beating a wild tattoo in her chest and she breathed shallowly, feeling as if she were standing on the edge of a precipice: behind her was the safety of returning to her own hotel suite, in front of her the unknown of sharing Lucien's bed for the night.

She drew in a shaky breath. 'Well, then...'

Lucien's control was now so tightly stretched that he felt as if the slightest provocation from Cyn would make it snap. That *he* would snap, and simply rip that T-shirt off her in the same way he had her blouse earlier.

It was an uncomfortable feeling for a man who never lost control. Of any situation and especially of himself. But this woman—barely tall enough to reach his shoulders, so slender he felt as if he might crush her if he held her too tightly—had thrown him off balance from the moment he first saw her.

Just twenty-four admittedly eventful hours ago...!

'Well, then…what…?' he prompted slowly.

The slenderness of Cyn's throat moved as she swallowed before answering him. 'Let's go to bed.'

'No more arguments or questions? Just "Let's go to bed"?' He raised dark brows.

She moistened her lips with the tip of her tongue before replying huskily. 'I—if that's okay with you, yes.'

If it was okay with him?

If Cyn only knew how much he wanted to rip her clothes off right now, before laying her down on the carpet and just taking her, right here and right now, plunging into the warmth of her again and again, then she would be probably be shocked out of her mind. *He* was out of his mind—for this woman.

Which was the reason Lucien was going to do none of those things. He was balanced on the edge of his self-control right now, and needed to slow things down. For Cyn's sake rather than his own. Because he didn't want to frighten her with the intensity of the desire she aroused in him.

'It's more than okay with me, Cyn,' he assured

her gruffly, blowing out the candles on the table and throwing the room into darkness before putting his arm about the slenderness of her waist as he guided her out of the dining room and down the hallway towards his bedroom.

Thia's nervousness deepened with each step she took down the hallway towards sharing Lucien's bed. To sharing Lucien Steele's bed!

Those other women—the ones she had seen online, photographed with Lucien—had all looked sophisticated and confident, and they no doubt had the physical experience, the confidence in their sexuality, to go with those looks. Whereas she—

For goodness' sake, she was twenty-three years old and she was going to lose her virginity some time—so why not with Lucien, a man she found as physically exciting as she did knee-meltingly attractive. A man who made her feel safe and protected as well as desired.

Was that *all* she felt for Lucien?

Or was she already a little—more than a little!—in love with him?

And wouldn't that be the biggest mistake of her life—in love with a man whose relationships never seemed to last longer than a month?

'Cyn?'

She blinked as she realised that while she had been so lost in thought they had already entered what must be the master bedroom—Lucien's bedroom. A huge four-poster bed dominated the shadowed room, and those shadows made it impossible for her to tell whether the black, white and chrome décor Lucien seemed to prefer had spilt over into his bedroom. The carpet beneath her feet was certainly dark, as were the curtains and the satin cover and cushions piled on the bed, but the actual colours eluded her in the darkness...

'Say now if you're feeling...less than sure about this,' Lucien prompted gruffly, his hands resting lightly on her waist as he turned her so that she was looking up at him.

The one thing Thia was totally sure about was that she wanted Lucien. Her body ached with that longing; her breasts were swollen and tingling, nipples hard and aroused, and there was a heated dampness between her thighs. At the same time she *so* didn't want to be a disappointment to him!

It would have been better if he had just made love to her right there in the dining room. If he hadn't given her time to think, to become so nervous.

But this was Lucien Steele, a man of sophistication and control. He wasn't the type of man to be so desperate for a woman he would rip her clothes off—well, apart from Thia's blouse earlier. But that had been an accident rather than passion! Or the type of man to make wild and desperate love to her.

Thia chewed worriedly on her bottom lip as she looked up into his hard and shadowed face, at those pale eyes glittering down at her intently in the darkness. 'I am a little nervous,' she admitted softly. 'I'm not as experienced as you are, and there have been all those other women for you—' She broke off as he placed silencing fingertips against her lips.

'I'm clean medically, if that's what's bothering you.'

'It isn't,' she assured him hastily, her cheeks

blushing a fiery-red. 'And I—I'm—er—clean too.' How could she be anything else when she had never been to bed with anyone?

He nodded abruptly. 'And that's the last time I want to talk about other people for either of us.'

'But—'

'Cyn, neither of us is experienced when it comes to each other.' He moved his hand to gently cup her cheek. 'Half the fun will be in learning which caress or touch pleases the other,' he added huskily.

Fun? Going to bed with a man, making love with him, was *fun?* Thia had never thought of it in quite that light before, but she had no reason to doubt what Lucien said. He had always been totally, bluntly honest when he spoke to her.

'You're right.' She shook off her feelings of nervousness and straightened determinedly. 'Is it okay if I just use the bathroom?'

'Of course.' Lucien released her before stepping back. 'Don't be long,' he added huskily as he opened the door to the adjoining bathroom and switched on the light for her.

Thia leant back weakly against the door the

moment it closed behind her and she was alone in the bathroom, her legs shaking so badly she could no longer stand without that support at her back.

Lucien stared at that closed bathroom door for several seconds after Cyn had closed it so firmly behind her, a frown darkening his brow as he considered her behaviour just now. She was more than just nervous. She seemed almost afraid. Just of him? Or of any man?

Why? Had something happened to her in the past? Maybe even with Miller? Something to make her nervous about going to bed with another man? It seemed highly possible, when she'd admitted she *had* been thinking of the other man when he'd called her on it a few minutes ago. It made Lucien wish now that he had given in to the impulse he'd had this morning to punch the other man in the face as Miller threw Cyn's belongings into her suitcase without so much as a thought or a question as to what was going to happen to her.

Whatever the reason for Cyn's nervousness,

Lucien didn't intend adding to it. He was glad now that he had shown such restraint a few minutes ago. He wanted to make slow and leisurely love to her, no matter the cost to his own self-control. Wanted to touch and pleasure Cyn until she could think of nothing else, no one else, but him and their lovemaking—

Lovemaking? Was he actually falling in love with Cyn?

It was an emotion he had always avoided in the past, and his choice of women—experienced and self-absorbed—was probably a reflection of that decision. Until now. Cyn was like no other woman he had ever known. And, yes, she was slipping—already *had* slipped?—beneath his defences.

None of which he wanted to explore too deeply right now.

Lucien crossed the bedroom to turn on the bedside lamp before turning back the bedcovers and quickly removing his clothes. His shaft bobbed achingly now that it was free of the confines of his denims.

He lingered beside the bed, looking down at

the black silk bedsheets as he imagined how right Cyn would look lying there, with that beautiful, pale, luminescent body spread out before him like a feast he wanted to gorge himself on. Just the thought of it was enough to cause his aching erection to throb eagerly, releasing pre-cum onto the bulbous tip before it spilt over and dripped slowly down his length.

Sweet heaven!

Lucien grasped his length before smoothing that liquid over it with the soft pad of his thumb, knowing he had never been this aroused before, this needy of any woman. Not in the way he now needed—desired—Cyn...

Thia studied herself critically in the mirror over the bathroom sink once she had taken her clothes off. Her face was pale, eyes fever-bright, her hair a silky black curtain across her bared shoulders. Her skin was smooth and unblemished, breasts firm and uptilting, tipped by engorged rosy-red nipples. Her waist was slender, hips flaring gently around the dark thatch of curls between her thighs, her legs long and slender.

She was as ready as she was ever going to be to walk out of here and go to bed with Lucien!

That courage didn't include walking out stark naked, though, and quickly she pulled on the black silk robe she had found hanging behind the bathroom door, tying the belt of what was obviously Lucien's own bathrobe tightly about the slenderness of her waist before taking a deep breath and opening the bathroom door, switching off the light...

Only to come to an abrupt halt in that doorway as she realised that Lucien had turned on a single lamp on the bedside table, allowing her to see that the bedroom was indeed decorated in those black, white and chrome colours Lucien favoured. Lucien himself was already lying in the bed, that bronzed chest bare, only a black silk sheet draped over him and concealing his lower body.

She had thought they would make love in the darkness—had imagined slipping almost anonymously beneath the bedcovers and then—

'Take off the robe, Cyn.'

She raised a startled gaze to Lucien and saw he

was leaning up on his elbow, causing the muscles to bulge in his arm, as he looked across at her with those glittering silver eyes. The darkness of his overlong hair was now tousled and falling rakishly over his forehead, probably after he had removed his T-shirt.

He was utterly beautiful in the same way that a deadly predator was beautiful—with all the power in that sleek and muscled body just waiting to be unleashed.

'I want to look at you,' he encouraged gruffly.

Thia's throat had gone so dry she could barely speak. 'Doesn't that work both ways?'

'Sure.' The intensity of his gaze never left hers as he slowly kicked down the black silk sheet.

Thia's breath caught in her throat and she could only stand and stare. At the width of his shoulders. At his muscled chest covered in that misting of dark hair. She could now see that it trailed down over his navel and grew thicker at the base of his arousal.

Oh. Good. Grief.

That was never going to fit inside her!

Lucien was a tall man, several inches over six

feet and his bronze-skinned body was deeply muscled, so it was no surprise that his aroused shaft was in perfect proportion to the rest of him—at least nine, possibly ten inches long, and so thick and wide Thia doubted her fingers would meet if she were to clasp them around it as she so longed, ached to do. Just as she longed to caress, to touch and become familiar with every perfect inch of him!

Even so, her wide gaze moved back unerringly to the heavy thrust of his arousal.

Maybe it was like those 'one size fits all' pairs of socks or gloves you could buy? Hadn't she read somewhere, in one of those sophisticated women's magazines often left lying around in a dentist's waiting room, that if a woman was prepared properly, with lots of foreplay, she was capable of stretching *down there,* accommodating any length or thickness—

'Cyn?'

Her startled gaze moved back up to Lucien's face and, her cheeks flamed with colour as she met the heat in his eyes. He looked across at her expectantly, his hand held out to her invitingly, obviously waiting for her to unfasten the robe and remove it completely before joining him in the bed...

CHAPTER EIGHT

LUCIEN TAMPED DOWN the urgency he felt to get out of bed and go to Cyn and instead waited patiently, allowing Cyn to take her time, to adjust. Allowing her to be the one to come *to* him.

They had all night—hours and hours for him to pleasure her into coming *for* him!

Right now her face was so pale that her ivory skin appeared almost translucent. Blue veins showed at the delicacy of her temples and her cobalt-blue eyes were dark and shadowed as she continued to look across at him, cheeks pale, her lips slightly parted, as if she were having trouble breathing.

'I'm starting to get a complex, Cyn,' he murmured ruefully.

Her startled gaze was quickly raised to his. 'You are…? But you're beautiful, Lucien,' she murmured huskily.

'So are you.' Lucien slowly lifted his arm to hold out his hand to her again, holding his breath as the nervousness in Cyn's gaze told him that she might turn tail and run if he made any sort of hasty move in her direction. Something he found surprisingly endearing rather than irritating.

Cyn was so different from the women he had been with in the past. Beautiful women, certainly, but it was usually a pampered and sometimes enhanced beauty, after hours spent at beauty salons and spas or beneath a plastic surgeon's knife. And all those women, without exception, had been confident of their perfectly toned bodies, of their sexual appeal.

Cyn, on the other hand, obviously had no time or money to spend at beauty salons or spas. The sleekness of her body was just as nature had intended it, as was her breathtaking beauty. A beauty that was all the more appealing because Cyn seemed so completely unaware of it, of its effect on him and every other man she came into contact with. The women in New York society might have no interest in furthering the acquaintance of student/waitress Cynthia Hammond from England, but Lucien very much doubted the men felt the same way!

And Lucien was the lucky man who had her all to himself—for tonight, at least...

Thia was frozen in place—couldn't move, couldn't speak, could only continue to stand in the bathroom doorway as she stared across at Lucien in mute appeal, inwardly cursing herself for her gauche behaviour but unable to do anything about it.

'Please, Cyn!' he said gruffly.

It was the aching need that deepened Lucien's voice to a growl which finally broke her out of that icy cage, causing Thia to take one step forward, and then another, until she finally stood beside the bed, allowing Lucien to reach out and enfold one of her trembling hands in his much warmer one.

He lifted it slowly to his lips, his gaze still holding hers as those lips grazed the back of her knuckles, tongue rasping, tasting. 'You are so very beautiful, Cyn.'

The warmth of his breath brushed lightly against

her over-sensitised skin. She swallowed. 'I believe you'll find the saying is *Beautiful as sin...*'

'Nothing could be as beautiful as you.' He gave a slow shake of his head.

At this moment in time, Thia finished ruefully inside her head. Right here and right now she had Lucien's complete attention. But tomorrow it would be different—

Oh, to hell with tomorrow!

For once in her carefully constructed life she was going to take not what was safe, or what she could afford, but what she *wanted.*

And tonight she so very much wanted to be here with Lucien.

She lowered her lashes and pulled her hand gently from his grasp, before moving to unfasten the belt of the robe, shrugging the black silk from her shoulders and hearing Lucien's breath catching in his throat as she allowed the robe to slide down her arms to fall onto the carpet at her feet. She was completely naked in front of him as she finally raised her lashes to look at him.

'You're exquisite,' Lucien groaned, taking the time to admire each and every curve and dip and hollow of her naked body before moving smoothly up onto his knees at the edge of the bed, nullifying the difference in their heights, putting his face on a level with hers as his arms moved about the slenderness of her waist.

Her hands moved up to clasp onto his shoulders as he pulled her in closer to him. Her skin felt so soft and she was so slender Lucien felt as if he could wrap his arms about her twice. His palms spread, fingers splayed across her shapely bottom, as he settled those slender curves into his much harder ones before touching his mouth lightly against hers.

Lucien moved his lips across her creamy soft cheek to the softness beneath her ear, along the column of her throat. The rasp of his tongue tasted the shady hollows at the base of her throat as one of his hands curled about the gentle thrust of her breast, the soft pad of his thumb unerringly finding, stroking the aroused nipple.

'Look at the two of us, Cyn,' he groaned throatily. 'See how beautiful we are together,' he encouraged as she looked down to where his hand cupped her breast. He looked at that contrast himself. Ivory and bronze...

Her skin looked so white against the natural bronze tone of Lucien's. Ice and fire. And fire invariably melted ice, didn't it?

Thia's inhibitions were melting, and her earlier apprehension along with it, as she twined her arms over those strong, muscled shoulders, her fingers becoming entangled in silky dark hair as she initiated a kiss between them this time— gentle at first, and then deeper, hungrier, as their passion flared out of control.

Lucien continued to kiss her even as Thia felt his arms move beneath her knees and about her shoulders. He lifted her easily up and onto the bed, lying her down almost reverently onto the black silk sheets before stretching his long length beside her, his gaze holding hers before his head lowered, lashes falling down against those hard cheekbones, and his lips parted. He drew her nipple into his mouth, gently suckling, licking that aroused nub, even as his hands caressed the ribcage beneath her breasts, the slender curve of her waist, before moving lower still.

Thia arched into his caresses as her nervousness faded completely and pleasure coursed through her—building, building, until she moved restlessly against him, needing more, wanting more. She was groaning low in her throat as she felt Lucien's fingers against the silky curls between her thighs, seeking and finding the nubbin hidden there and moving lower still, to where the slickness of her juices had made her wet, so very wet, circling, moistening her swollen lips.

His thumb pressed delicately against the nubbin above and still she wanted more, needed more. She felt as if she were poised on the edge of a precipice, one that burned. Flames were licking up and through her body, sensitising her to every touch of Lucien's hands, to every sweep of his tongue across the swollen hardness of her nipples, as he divided his attentions between the two, first licking, then suckling. Each lick and suck seemed to increase the volcanic pleasure rising between her thighs.

'Please, Lucien!' Her fingers tightened in his hair and she pulled his head up, forced him to look at her with eyes that glittered pure silver. His lips were swollen and moist. 'Please...!' she groaned beseechingly. 'Lucien...'

He moved so swiftly, so urgently, that Thia barely had time to realise he now lay between her parted thighs.

'You are so beautiful *here,* Cyn,' he murmured. His breath was a warm caress as the soft pads of his thumbs slicked her juices over those plump folds and the sensitive knot of flesh above. 'Look at us, Cyn,' he encouraged gruffly. 'Move up onto your elbows and show me those pretty breasts.'

Thia would have done anything Lucien asked of her at that moment. Her cheeks were flushed, eyes fever-bright, as she looked down at him, at his hair midnight-black against the paleness of her skin, bronzed back long and muscled, buttocks taut.

His gaze held hers as he cupped his hands beneath her bottom and held her up and open to him. 'I'm going to eat you up, Cyn,' he promised, and his head lowered and his tongue swept, rasped against her slick folds.

Over and over again he lapped her gently, and then harder, until Thia was no longer able to hold herself up on her elbows as the pleasure grew and grew inside her. Lucien's fingers were digging almost painfully into the globes of her bottom as he thrust a tongue deep inside her slick channel, sending her over that volcanic edge as the pleasure surged and swelled, surged and swelled again and again, taking Thia into the magic of her first ever climax.

It was the first of many. Lucien continued to pleasure her, taking her up to that plateau again and again, each time ensuring that he took her over the edge and into the maelstrom of pleasure on the other side, until Thia's throat felt ragged and sore from the sobbing cries of each climax. Her body was becoming completely boneless as those releases came swifter and fiercer each time, and Lucien's arms were looped beneath her thighs now, holding her wider to allow for the ministrations of his lips and tongue, increasing her pleasure each and every time she came.

'No more, Lucien!' Thia finally gasped, her fingers digging into his muscled shoulders. Blackness had begun to creep into the edges of her vision and she knew she couldn't take any more. There was foreplay and then there was hurtling over the edge into unconsciousness. Which was exactly what was going to happen if her body was racked by one more incredible climax! 'Please, Lucien. I just can't...' She looked at him pleadingly as he raised his head to look at her, his cheeks flushed, lips swollen and moist.

'I'm sorry—I got carried away. Are you okay?' He gave a shake of his head.

'Yes...'

'You just taste so delicious...' He groaned achingly as he moved up beside her, his hands shaking slightly as he cupped the heat of her cheek. 'Like the finest, rarest brandy. I just couldn't stop drinking your sweet essence. Taste yourself, Cyn,' he encouraged huskily, and brushed his lips lightly against hers.

The taste was sweet and slightly salty, with an underlying musk. Thia's cheeks blazed with colour at the knowledge that Lucien now knew her body inside and out, more intimately than she did. That he—

She tensed to stillness as the telephone began to ring on the bedside table. Lucien scowled his displeasure and didn't even glance at the telephone. 'Ignore it,' he rasped.

'But—'

'Nothing and no one is going to intrude on the two of us being together tonight. I won't allow it,' he stated determinedly.

'But it could be important—'

'Obviously not,' he murmured in satisfaction as the telephone fell quiet after the sixth ring, allowing him to reach out and remove the receiver to prevent it from ringing and disturbing them again.

He rolled onto his back, hands firm on Cyn's hips, and lifted her up and over him. Her thighs now straddled his, and the dampness of her folds pressed against the hardness of his shaft as she sat upright, the swell of her breasts, tipped by strawberry-ripe nipples, peeping through the dark swathe of her hair.

'Do you have birth control, Cyn?'

'I didn't think…' she groaned. 'I—no, I don't.' Her cheeks were fiery red. 'Do you?'

Lucien would have preferred there to be nothing between him and Cyn the first time he entered her, but at the same time he liked that her lack of protection indicated she wasn't involved sexually with any other man right now.

He reached out and opened a drawer on the side table before taking out a silver foil packet and opening it. 'Would you…?' he invited huskily.

'Me?' Her eyes were wide.

'Perhaps not.' Lucien chuckled softly before quickly dealing with it himself. 'I want to be inside you now, Cyn…' he said huskily. 'In fact if I don't get inside you soon I think I'm going to spontaneously combust.' He settled her above him. 'I promise I'll go slower next time, but for the moment I just need—'

'Next time…?' Cyn squeaked.

'You said earlier that you would stay with me until I had made love to you half a dozen times, remember?' Lucien gave a hard, satisfied smile.

She gasped. 'But I—I already—I've lost count of how many times I've already—'

'Foreplay doesn't count,' he dismissed. 'When I'm inside you and we climax together—something I'm greatly looking forward to, by the way—that's when it counts. And I want you so

badly this time I'm not going to last,' he acknowledged.

He knew it was true. His liking for Cyn, his
enjoyment of her company as well as her body,
had enhanced their lovemaking to a pitch he had
never known before...

Thia gasped. All those incredible, mind-blowing climaxes didn't *count?* He couldn't truly
think that she was going to be able to repeat this
past hour—or however long it had been since
Lucien had started making love to her. She
had completely lost track of time! If they did
she wouldn't just lose consciousness, she would
surely die. And wouldn't that look great on her
headstone—*Here lies Cynthia Hammond, dead
from too much pleasure!*

But what a wonderful way to go...

Emotion—love...?—swelled in Thia's chest as
she looked down at the man sprawled beneath her
on the bed. Lucien really was the most gorgeous,
sexy man she had ever met—breathtakingly
handsome, elegantly muscled and loose-limbed.
And he was all hers.

For the moment, that taunting little voice whispered again inside her head.

This moment was all that mattered. Because it was all there was for her and Lucien. They had no tomorrow. No future. Just here and now.

And she wanted it. Wanted Lucien.

She held that silver gaze with her own and eased up on her knees before reaching down between them, fingers light, as she guided his sheathed length to the slickness of her channel—only to freeze in place as she suddenly heard the unexpected sound of Mozart's *Requiem* playing!

'It's my mobile,' Lucien explained impatiently when he saw Cyn's dazed expression. 'Damn, it!' His hands slapped down forcefully onto the mattress beside him. He should have turned the damn thing off before making love with Cyn. Should have—

'You need to answer it, Lucien.' A frown marred Cyn's brow. 'It must be something important for someone to call again so quickly—and on your mobile this time.'

Nothing was more important at this moment than his need to make love with Cyn. *Nothing!*

'Lucien...?' she prompted huskily as his damned mobile just kept on playing Mozart's *Requiem*.

Which, in the circumstances, was very apt...

Talk about killing the moment! One interruption was bad enough. Lucien had managed to save the situation the first time, but he doubted he would be able to do so a second time.

A sentiment Cyn obviously echoed as she slid off and away from him, over to the side of the bed, before bending down to pick up the black silk robe from the floor. Her back was long and slender, ivory skin gleaming pale and oh-so-beautiful in the glow of the lamp, before she slipped her arms into the robe, pulling it about herself and then standing up to fasten the belt. She turned to face him.

'You have to answer the call, Lucien.' Her gaze remained firmly fixed on his face rather than lower, where he was still hard and wanting.

Oh, yes, there was no doubting he had to answer the call—and whoever was on the other end of it was going to feel the full force of his displeasure!

He slid to the side of the bed before reaching for his denims and taking his mobile out of the pocket to take the call. 'Steele,' he rasped harshly.

Thia winced at the coldness of Lucien's voice, feeling sorry for whoever was on the other end of that line. At the same time she couldn't help but admire the play of muscles across the broad width of Lucien's shoulders and back beneath that bronzed skin as he sat on the other side of the bed, his black hair rakishly tousled from her fingers earlier.

Earlier...

Her cheeks warmed as she thought of those earlier intimacies. Lucien's hands, lips and tongue caressing her, touching her everywhere. Giving pleasure wherever they touched. Taking her to climax again and again.

Her legs trembled just at remembering that pleasure—

'I'll be down in five minutes,' Lucien grated harshly, before abruptly ending the call and standing up decisively to cross the room and collect up the clothes he had taken off earlier, his eyes cold, his expression grimly discouraging.

Thia looked at him dazedly. He seemed almost unaware of her presence. 'Lucien...?'

He was scowling darkly as he turned to look at her. 'That was Dex,' he bit out economically. 'It appears that your ex-boyfriend is downstairs in Reception and he's been making a damned exhibition of himself!'

She gasped. 'Jonathan?'

Lucien nodded sharply. 'Unless you have any other ex-boyfriends in New York?'

She gave a pained wince at the harsh anger she heard in his tone. Misdirected anger, in her opinion. 'I told you—Jonathan was never my boyfriend. And isn't it more likely he's making an exhibition of himself in *your* hotel because you fired him from *Network* this morning?'

It was a valid, reasoned argument, Lucien acknowledged impatiently—but at the same time he knew he was just too tense at the moment to be reasoned with. Even by Cyn.

He had enjoyed this evening with her more than he had enjoyed being with a woman for a very long time—if ever. Not just making love to her, but cooking dinner with her, talking freely about everything and nothing, when usually he was careful of how much he revealed about himself to the women he was involved with—a self-defence reflex that simply hadn't existed with Cyn from the beginning.

And now *this*.

His mouth thinned with his displeasure. 'I apologise for being grouchy. I just—' He ran his hand through the dark thickness of his hair. 'I'll get dressed and go down and sort this situation out. I shouldn't be long. What are you doing...?' He frowned as Cyn turned towards the bathroom.

'Getting dressed so that I can come with you.'

'You aren't coming downstairs with me.'

'Oh, but I am,' she assured him.

'No—'

'Yes,' she bit out firmly, her hands resting on her hips as she raised challenging brows.

Lucien's nostrils flared. 'My hotel. My problem.'

'Your hotel, certainly. But we don't know yet whose problem it is,' she insisted stubbornly.

His jaw clenched. 'Look, Cyn, there are some things about Miller I don't believe you're aware of—'

'What sort of things?' She looked at him sharply.

'Things,' Lucien bit out tersely. This evening had already gone to hell in a handbasket. Cyn did not need to know about all of Jonathan Miller's behaviour, or the reason the other man had been using her, which was sure to come out if Miller was as belligerent as Dex had said he was. 'In the circumstances, the best thing you can do is—'

'Please don't tell me that the best thing I can do is to stay up here and make coffee, like a good little woman, and wait until the Mighty Hunter returns!' Her eyes glowed deeply cobalt.

Apart from the good little woman and Mighty Hunter crack, that was exactly what Lucien had been about to say. 'Well…maybe you could forget the coffee,' he said dryly.

'And maybe I can forget the whole scenario— because it isn't going to happen!' She thrust her hands into the pockets of his silk robe.

Lucien noted that it was far too big for her; it

was wrapped about her almost twice, with the sleeves turned up to the slenderness of her wrists, and the length reached down to her calves—altogether making her look like a little girl trying to play grown-up.

'Dex has managed to take Miller to a secure room for the moment, but it could get nasty, Cyn.'

'I've been a waitress for six years; believe me, I know how to deal with *nasty*,' she assured him dryly.

Lucien was starting to notice that Cyn seemed to use the waitress angle as a defence mechanism. As if in constant reminder to herself, and more probably Lucien, of who and what she was...

Who she was to Lucien was Cynthia Hammond—a beautiful and independent young woman whom he admired and desired.

What she was to Lucien was also Cynthia Hammond—a beautiful and independent young woman whom Lucien admired as well as desired.

The rest, he realised, had become totally unimportant to him—was just background noise and of no consequence.

Not true of Cyn, obviously...

He drew in a deep breath. 'I would really rather you didn't do this.'

'Your opinion is noted.' She nodded.

'But ignored?'

'But ignored.'

'Fine,' he bit out between clenched teeth, knowing he couldn't like Cyn's independence of spirit on the one hand and then expect her not to do exactly as she pleased on the other. 'I'll be leaving in about two minutes. If you aren't ready—'

'I'll be ready.'

She hurried into the bathroom and closed the door behind her.

Lucien drew in several controlling breaths as he glared at that closed bathroom door, knowing that the next few minutes' conversation with Miller would in all probability put an end to Lucien and Cyn spending the rest of the night together...

CHAPTER NINE

'MAKING AN EXHIBITION of himself how?' Thia prompted softly.

Lucien was scowling broodingly where he stood on the other side of the private lift as it descended to the ground floor.

He was once again dressed in those casual denims and black T-shirt, although the heavy darkness of his hair was still tousled—from Thia's own fingers earlier, and also Lucien's own now as he ran his hands through it in impatient frustration. Probably because of her stubbornness in insisting on accompanying him downstairs rather than Jonathan's behaviour, Thia acknowledged ruefully.

Silver eyes glittered through narrowed lids. 'He came in and demanded to see me. According to Dex, once both the receptionist and the manager had told him I wasn't available this evening,

Miller then decided to start shouting and hurling the potted plants about. When that failed to get him what he wanted he resorted to smashing up the furniture, which was when Security arrived and took charge of the situation.'

'How...?'

'Two of them lifted him up and carried him away to a secure room before calling Dex,' Lucien explained grimly.

Thia winced as she pictured the scene. 'I can imagine Jonathan might be upset after what happened this morning, but surely this isn't normal behaviour?'

Lucien gave her an irritated frowning glance. 'Cyn, have you *really* not noticed anything different about him since you came to New York?'

Well...she *had* noticed that Jonathan was more self-absorbed than he'd used to be. That he slept the mornings away and barely spoke when he did emerge, sleepy-eyed and unkempt, from his bedroom. And he had insisted on the two of them attending those awful parties together every night, at which he usually abandoned her shortly after they had arrived. And he had been extremely aggressive at the Carews' party last night—she had the sore wrist and the bruises on her arms to prove that!

She chewed on her bottom lip. 'Maybe he's a little more…into himself than he used to be.'

'That's one way of describing it, I suppose.' Lucien nodded grimly, standing back as the lift came to a halt and allowing her to step out into the marbled hallway first.

Thia eyed him guardedly as she walked along the hallway beside him; Lucien obviously knew which room Jonathan had been secured in. 'How would *you* describe it?'

Lucien's mouth thinned. 'As the classic behaviour of an addict.'

She drew in a sharp breath as she came to an abrupt halt in the hallway. 'Are you saying that Jonathan is—that he's taking drugs?'

'Amongst other things.' Lucien scowled.

'He's drinking too?'

'Not that I know of, no.'

'Then what "other things" are you talking about…?' Thia felt dazed, disorientated, at Lucien's revelation about Jonathan. Admittedly

Jonathan hadn't seemed quite himself since she arrived in New York, but she had put that down to reaction to his sudden stardom. It must be difficult coping with being so suddenly thrust into the limelight, finding himself so much in demand, as well as having so many beautiful women throwing themselves at him.

Lucien grimaced. 'This is not a good time for me to discuss this with you.'

'It's exactly the time you should discuss this with me,' Thia insisted impatiently. 'Maybe if someone had thought to discuss it with me earlier I might have been able to talk to him about it— perhaps persuaded him to seek help.' She gave a shake of her head. 'As things now stand he's not only messed up his career, but the rest of his life as well!'

Lucien frowned as he heard the underlying criticism in her tone. 'Damn it, Cyn, do *not* turn this around on me. Miller was given a warning about his behaviour weeks ago. In fact he's been given two warnings.'

'When, exactly?'

'The first was two months ago. And again

about five weeks ago, when it became obvious
he had taken no notice of the first warning. I
have a strict no-drugs policy on all contracts,'
he added grimly.

'What sort of warn—? Did you say *five weeks*
ago…?' she prompted guardedly.

Lucien quirked dark brows. 'Mean something
to you?'

'Jonathan visited me in London a month ago…'
She chewed on her bottom lip. 'I hadn't seen him
for almost three months, and he had only telephoned me a couple of times since he'd left for
New York, and then he—he just turned up one
weekend.'

Lucien nodded. 'And subsequently invited you
to come and stay with him in New York?'

'How do you know that?'

He scowled. 'I just did the math, Cyn.'

'I don't understand…'

Lucien didn't see why he should be the one to
explain Miller's behaviour, either. Cyn already
considered him callous for firing Miller. He
wasn't going to be the one to tell her that Miller

had only invited her to New York as a cover for his affair with another—married!—woman!

The fact that Cyn was with him now would probably be enough for Miller to realise she must have been with Lucien in his apartment when Dex telephoned a short time ago. Add that to the fact that she was so obviously wearing a man's oversized T-shirt and Miller was sure to add two and two together and come up with the correct answer of four!

Which was precisely the reason Lucien hadn't wanted Cyn with him during this confrontation. Well, okay, it wasn't the whole reason. He really would have preferred it that Cyn stayed in his apartment, made coffee, like the good little woman, and waited for the Mighty Hunter to return. He wanted to protect her from herself, if necessary. As it was, he somehow doubted that Cyn would be returning to his apartment tonight at all...

'Could we get a move on, do you think?' Lucien snapped tersely, giving a pointed glance at his wristwatch. 'I told Dex I'd be there in five minutes and it's been over ten.'

Cyn blinked at his vehemence. 'Of course. Sorry.'

She grimaced as she once again fell into step beside him, leaving Lucien feeling as if he had just delivered a kick to an already abused and defenceless animal.

Not that he thought of Cyn as defenceless— she was too independent, too determined ever to be completely that. But he had no doubt that Miller's real reason for inviting her to come to New York was going to upset her.

It was hard to believe, considering the tension between them now, that the two of them had been making love just minutes ago—that he now knew Cyn's body intimately, and exactly how to give her pleasure.

On the plus side, his erection had got the message that the night of pleasure was over and had deflated back to normal proportions. Not that it would take much to revive his desire...just a sultry look from cobalt blue eyes, the merest touch of Cyn's hand anywhere on his body. Which Lucien already knew wasn't going to happen in the immediate future. If ever again.

Another reason for Lucien to be displeased at Miller's increasingly erratic behaviour. If he needed another reason. Which he didn't. Forget the drugs and the affair with Simone Carew; the man was an out-and-out bastard for attempting to use Cyn as a shield for that affair. Not that the ruse had worked, but that didn't excuse Miller's callous behaviour towards a woman who had thought he was her friend. Or the fact that the other man had held Cyn so roughly the evening before he had succeeded in badly bruising her.

And Cyn was annoyed with *him*, because he had fired Miller for blatant and continuous breach of contract!

'Dex.' He greeted the other man grimly as they turned a corner and he saw his bodyguard standing outside a door to the right of the hallway. 'He's in there?' He nodded to the closed door.

Dex scowled. 'Yes.'

'And has he quietened down?'

'Some.' Dex nodded grimly before shooting Cyn a frowning glance. 'I don't think it's a good idea for Miss Hammond to go in with you. Miller is violent, and he's also throwing out all sorts of accusations,' he warned with a pointed glance at Lucien.

'I'm going in,' Cyn informed them both stubbornly.

Lucien's mouth tightened. 'As you can see, Dex, Miss Hammond insists on accompanying me.'

'It's really not a good idea, Miss Hammond,' Dex warned her gently.

It was a gentleness Lucien hadn't even known the other man was capable of. No doubt Dex found Cyn's beauty and her air of fragility appealing—but the fragility was deceptive. There was a toughness beneath that fragile exterior that made Lucien think Cyn would be capable of stopping a Humber in its tracks if she chose to do so! Hopefully Dex was concerned in a fatherly sort of way, because Lucien knew he wouldn't be at all happy with his bodyguard having a crush on the woman he—

The woman he what...? Was falling in love with? Was already in love with?

Now was hardly the time for Lucien to think about what he might or might not be feeling for Cyn. Damn it, they had met precisely three times now, and shared one evening together. Admittedly it had been the most enjoyable—and arousing!—evening Lucien had ever spent with a woman...

The depth of his desire for Cyn was unprecedented—to the point that Lucien really had thought he was going to come just at the taste of her on his tongue.

And for the early part of the evening she had believed him to have deliberately hidden her away in his apartment because he didn't want to be seen in public with her. She may still believe that, for all he had denied it.

Damn it, he should have tanned her backside earlier rather than making love to her!

'I appreciate your concern, Dex.' Thia answered the older man softly. 'But Jonathan is my friend—'

'No. He really isn't,' Lucien rasped harshly.

'And I have every intention of speaking with him tonight,' she continued firmly, at the same time giving Lucien a reproving frown.

'I agree with Mr Steele,' Dex murmured regretfully. 'Mr Miller's behaviour earlier was…out of control,' he added.

Thia had come to like and trust this man over the past couple of days—how could she *not* like and trust a man who had stood guard all night outside her bedroom in that awful hotel in order to ensure she came to no harm from any of the staff or other guests staying there? In fact she felt slightly guilty now, for thinking Dex looked like a thug the first time she had seen him. He might look tough, but she didn't doubt there was a heart of gold under that hard exterior.

And she valued his advice now—as she did Lucien's. Although his scowling expression indicated he thought otherwise! She just didn't feel she could abandon Jonathan when he so obviously needed all the friends he could get. She had no doubt that all those shallow people who had been all over Jonathan at those celebrity parties would drift away the moment they knew he had been dropped as the star of *Network*.

'I appreciate your concern, Dex.' She smiled her gratitude as she placed a hand lightly on his muscled forearm. 'I really do.'

'But she's going to ignore it,' Lucien said knowingly.

Her smile faded as she turned to face him, knowing how displeased he was with her by the coldness in his eyes as he looked down the length of his nose at her, but unable to do anything about it.

She accepted, despite that interruption to their lovemaking, that Lucien had become her lover this evening—was closer to her and now knew her more intimately than any other man ever had. But by the same token she had been friends with Jonathan for two years now, and she didn't desert her friends. Especially when one of those friends was so obviously in trouble.

She drew in a deep, steadying breath. 'Yes, I'm afraid I am.'

Lucien had known she would. She had to be the most irritatingly stubborn woman he had ever known!

As well as being the most beautiful—inside as well as out. And the funniest. Her comments were sometimes totally outrageous. She was also the sexiest woman Lucien had ever known. And definitely the most responsive!

That in itself was such a turn-on—an aphrodisiac. Lucien was an accomplished lover, and had certainly never had any complaints about his sexual technique, his ability to bring a woman to climax, or in finding his own release. But with Cyn there had been no need for that measured and deliberate technique—just pure pleasure as, after her initial shyness, she had held absolutely nothing back and responded to his lightest touch, at the same time heightening his own pleasure and arousal.

To such an extent that Lucien knew Cyn was fast becoming his own addiction...

And yet here they were at loggerheads again, just minutes later—and over Jonathan Miller, of all people. A man Lucien didn't consider as being good enough to lick Cyn's boots, let alone to deserve her loyalty and friendship.

'Fine,' he bit out harshly before turning away. 'You had better unlock the door and let us in, then, Dex. The sooner we get this over and done with the better for all of us,' he added grimly.

'Lucien...?' Cyn prompted almost pleadingly.

'You've made your decision, Cyn.' He rounded on her angrily, hands clenching at his sides. 'I only hope you don't live to regret it. No, damn it, I *know* you're going to regret it!' He glared down at her.

Thia had a sinking feeling she would too... Both Dex and Lucien seemed convinced of it, and she had no reason to distrust the opinion of either man.

Yes, Jonathan had been less than a polite host since she'd arrived in New York—to the point where his behaviour the previous evening meant she'd had no choice but to move out of his apartment. She just couldn't quite bring herself to turn her back on him if he needed a friend.

Lucien followed Dex into the room, the two of them blocking her view of Jonathan until they moved aside and Thia finally saw him where he stood silhouetted against the darkness of the window. He looked a mess: his denims were covered in soil—from the pot plants he had thrown about the hotel reception?—his T-shirt was ragged and torn, but it was the bruises on his face and the cut over one eye that dismayed her the most.

His lips curled back into a sneer as he saw the shocked expression on her face. 'You should see the other guy!'

'The "other guy" is at the hospital, having stitches put in the gash to the head he received when you smashed a lamp over him,' Lucien rasped harshly.

Jonathan turned that sneering expression onto the older man. 'He shouldn't have got in my way.'

'Watch your mouth, Miller. Unless you want him to press charges for assault,' Lucien warned grimly.

Thia paled at the knowledge that Jonathan had attacked another man with a lamp, necessitating that man needing to go to the hospital for stitches. 'You're just making the situation worse, Jonathan—'

'Exactly what are *you* doing here, Thia?' Jonathan turned on her, eyeing her speculatively as he took in the whole of her appearance in one sweeping glance. 'You look as if you just fell out of bed. Oh. My. God.' He gave a harsh laugh as he turned that speculative gaze on Lucien and then back to Thia. 'You just fell out of *his* bed! How priceless is that—'

She winced. 'Jonathan, don't.'

'Shut up, Miller,' Lucien bit out coldly at the same time.

'The prudish Thia Hammond and the almighty Lucien Steele!' Jonathan ignored them both as he laughed all the harder at a joke obviously only he appreciated.

Thia felt numb. Lucien was obviously icily furious. Dex remained stoically silent.

Jonathan's humour was so derisive and scathing Thia felt about two inches high—as he no doubt intended her to do. 'You aren't helping, Jonathan.'

'I have nothing left to lose,' he assured her scornfully as he gave a shake of his head. 'You stupid little fool—don't you know that he's just using you to get back at me?' He looked at Thia pityingly.

'You're the one who used her, Miller,' Lucien scorned icily.

Jonathan glared. 'I tried to convince you that Thia and I were involved, yes. In the futile hope of getting you off my back. But what you've done tonight—seducing Thia—is ten times worse than anything I did!' He gave a disgusted shake of his head before turning to Thia with accusing eyes. 'Damn it, Thia, we actually dated for a while two years ago—until you made it obvious you weren't interested in me in that way. And yet you only met Steele yesterday and already you've been to bed with him! Un-bloody-believable!' He eyed her incredulously.

When he put it like that it *was* pretty incredible, Thia acknowledged with an inner wince. Not that she and Lucien had completely consummated their lovemaking, but that was pure semantics. After the number of times Lucien had brought her to sobbing orgasm he was definitely her lover. A man, as Jonathan had just pointed out, she had only known for twenty-four hours...

Lucien had heard enough—seen enough. Cyn's face was tinged slightly green and she was swaying slightly, as if she was about to pass out! 'I suggest we talk about this again tomorrow, Miller,' he snapped icily. 'When you've had a chance to...calm down.' He eyed the other man disgustedly, knowing by Miller's flushed cheeks and over-bright eyes that he was high on something—something he needed to sleep off overnight. Preferably with Dex keeping a sharp eye on him to ensure he didn't take anything else.

'You would no doubt prefer it if Thia didn't hear all the sordid details?' the younger man taunted.

Lucien shrugged. 'They're your sordid details.'

'Not all of them,' Miller challenged. 'Something I'm pretty sure you won't have shared with Thia either.'

Lucien's mouth tightened. 'Not only do your empty threats carry no weight with me, but they could be decidedly dangerous. To your future career,' he added softly.

'You don't think Thia has a right to know that the *real* reason you've been trying to break my contract the last couple of months—the reason for your being with her tonight—is because I've been having an affair with the woman I seduced out of *your* bed?'

'We both know that isn't true, Miller.' Lucien's teeth were clenched so tightly his jaw ached.

'Do we?'

'Yes!' he rasped. 'Something I will discuss with you in more detail tomorrow,' he added determinedly.

'And will you also fill me in on all the juicy details of how you succeeded in seducing and deflowering the Virgin Queen?' Miller came back tauntingly.

'What the hell…?' Lucien muttered.

'It's what I've always called Thia in my mind.' The other man grinned unrepentantly.

Lucien stilled as all thought of Miller's accusations fled his mind. Barely breathing, he felt his heart pounding loudly in his chest as he gave Cyn a brief disbelieving glance—just long enough to show him that she had somehow managed to go even paler. Her cheeks were now paper-white.

The Virgin Queen?

Was it possible that on this subject at least Miller might be telling the truth and Cyn had been a virgin? Correction: she was still technically a virgin—despite the intensity of their lovemaking earlier.

Had Lucien taken a virgin to his bed and not

even known it? Would he only have realised it the moment he ripped through that delicate barrier?

Lucien was the one who now felt nauseous. Sick to his stomach, in fact, at how close he had come to taking Cyn's innocence without even realising until it was too late.

Perhaps he should have known.

He had noted that disingenuous air about her the first time they met. There had also been her shyness earlier, in regard to her own nudity as much as his. Her confusion when he had assured her he had a clean bill of health and her hesitant confirmation that she did too. And the glaringly obvious fact that Cyn wasn't on any birth control.

Because she was a virgin.

Even during the wildness of his youth Lucien had never taken a virgin to his bed—had stayed well away from any female who looked as if she might still be one. A woman's virginity was something to be valued—a gift—not something to be thrown away on a casual relationship, and Lucien had never felt enough for any of the women he had been involved with to want to take a relationship any further.

What had Cyn been thinking earlier?

Maybe she hadn't been thinking at all? Lucien knew he certainly hadn't. He had been too aroused, too caught up in the intensity of his desire for Cyn—of his growing addiction to her—to be able to connect up the dots of her behaviour and their conversation and realise exactly how innocent she was. As it was, he had been on the point of thrusting into her, of taking her innocence, when the ringtone of his mobile had interrupted them.

Sweet, merciful heaven…!

CHAPTER TEN

'LUCIEN—'

'Not now, Thia.'

She almost had to run to keep up with Lucien's much longer strides, and Jonathan's mocking laughter followed them as they walked down the deserted marble hallway towards where the main lifts were situated, in the reception area of the hotel. The lifts Thia would need to use if she was returning to her suite on the tenth floor. Which it seemed she was about to do...

'Is Dex going to stay with Jonathan tonight?' Thia hadn't been able to hear all the softly spoken conversation that had taken place between Lucien and Dex before Lucien had taken a firm hold of her arm and escorted her from the room, but she had gathered that Dex intended taking Jonathan out of the back entrance of the hotel and then driving him to his apartment.

Lucien nodded abruptly. 'If only to make sure he stays out of trouble for the rest of the night.'

She winced. 'Is the drug thing really that bad?'

'Yes,' he answered grimly.

Thia frowned. 'Lucien, what did Jonathan mean? He seemed to be implying that there was a woman involved in your decision to fire him from *Network*?'

Lucien turned to look down at her with icy silver eyes. 'I don't think that's the conversation we should be having right now, Thia.'

The fact that he kept calling her Thia in that icily clipped tone was far from reassuring... Not that she wasn't totally aware of the reason for Lucien's coldness. It was as if an arctic chill had taken over the room the moment Jonathan had so baldly announced her virginity. Lucien's shocked reaction to that statement had been unmistakable. As if she had a disease, or something equally as unpleasant! Good grief, he had been a virgin himself once upon a time—many years ago now, no doubt, but still...

'I don't understand why you're so annoyed.' She frowned. 'It's my virginity, and as such I can choose to lose it when I damn well please. It's no big deal.'

'I'm guessing that's why you've waited twenty-three years to even think about doing so?'

Thia smarted at his scathing tone. 'It isn't the first time I've considered it—and that's my bruised arm, Lucien!' she complained, when his fingers tightly grasped the top of her arm as he came to a halt in the deserted hallway before swinging her round to face him.

He released her as abruptly, glaring down at her, nostrils flaring as he breathed deeply. 'What the hell were you thinking, Thia? What were you doing going alone to a man's apartment at all?'

'Accepting an invitation to dinner in a man's apartment isn't saying *Here I am—take me to bed!*'

'It's been my experience that that depends on the woman and her reasons for accepting the invitation.'

She bristled. 'I don't think I like the accusation in your tone.'

'Well, that's just too bad,' he bit out harshly. 'Because my tone isn't going to change until I know exactly why you went to bed with me earlier this evening!'

Her cheeks blazed with colour. 'I thought I was making love with a man whom I desired and who also desired me!'

His jaw tightened. 'Not good enough, Thia—'

'Well, it's the only explanation I have. And stop calling me that!' Tears stung her eyes.

'It's your name,' he dismissed curtly.

'But *you've* never called me by it.' She blinked back those heated tears. 'And I—I liked it that only you had ever called me Cyn,' she admitted huskily, realising it was the truth. She had found Lucien's unique name for her irritating at first, but had very quickly come to like that uniqueness.

His nostrils flared in his impatience. 'Answer the damned question, Thia!'

'Which one?' she came back just as angrily. He'd called her that name again. 'Why did I decide to have dinner alone with you in your apartment this evening? Or why did I choose you as the man to whom I wanted to lose my virginity? Or perhaps to you they're one and the same question?' she challenged scornfully. 'You obviously think that I had pre-planned going to bed with you this evening! That I was attempting to—to entrap you into—into *what,* exactly?' Thia looked at him sharply.

Lucien was still too stunned at the knowledge of Cyn's virginity—at the thought of her never having been with anyone else—to be able to reason this situation out with his usually controlled logic. As a consequence he was talking without thinking about what he was saying, uncharacteristically shooting straight from the hip. But, damn it, if his mobile had rung even a few seconds later—!

'Damned if I know,' he muttered exasperatedly.

'Oh, I think you *do* know, Lucien.' Cyn's voice shook with anger. 'I think you've decided—that you believe—I deliberately set out to seduce you this evening.'

'I believe *I* was the one who did the seducing—'

'Ah, but what if I'm clever enough to let you *think* you did the seducing?' she taunted, eyes glittering darkly.

He gave a rueful shake of his head. 'You aren't—'

'It's a pity you asked about birth control, really,' she continued without pause. 'Otherwise I might even have discovered I was pregnant in a few weeks' time. And wouldn't that have been wonderful? I can see the headlines in the newspapers now—*I had Lucien Steele's love-child!* Except we aren't in love with each other, and there isn't ever going to be a child—'

'Stop it, Cyn!' he rasped sharply, reaching up to grasp her by the shoulders before shaking her. 'Just *stop* it!'

'Let me go, Lucien,' she choked. 'I don't like you very much at the moment.' Tears fell unchecked down the paleness of her cheeks, her eyes dark blue pools of misery.

Lucien didn't like himself very much at the moment either. And it was really no excuse that he was still in shock from Miller's 'Virgin Queen' comment. His knee-jerk angry comments had now made Cyn think—believe—that he was angry about her virginity. When in actual fact he felt like getting down on his knees and worshipping at her beautiful feet. A woman's virginity was a gift. A gift Cyn had been about to give to *him* this evening. The truth was he was in total awe at the measure of that gift.

And he had made her cry. That was just unacceptable.

He released her shoulders before pulling her into his arms—a move she instantly fought against as she tried to push him away, before beating her fists against his chest when she failed to release herself.

'I said, let me go, Lucien!' She glared up at him as he still held her tightly against his chest.

'Let me explain, Cyn—'

'I have questions I want answered too, Lucien. And so far you've refused to answer any of them. Including explaining about this woman Jonathan reputedly stole from you—'

'I don't consider Miller's fantasies as being relevant to our present conversation!' He scowled darkly.

'And I disagree with that opinion. Jonathan said that the two of us making love together this eve-

ning was deliberate on your part—that you seduced me to get back at him—'

'Does that *really* sound like something I would
do?' he grated, jaw clenched.

'Any more than entrapment sounds like something I would do?' she came back tauntingly. 'I
don't really know you, Lucien…'

'Oh, you know me, Cyn,' Lucien assured her
softly. 'In just a few short days I've allowed you
to know me better than anyone else ever has. And
the conversation we need to have is about what
happened between the two of us this evening.'

'I think we—you, certainly—have already said
more than enough on that subject!' she assured
him firmly.

'Because I was understandably stunned at
learning of your—your innocence?'

'Was that you being stunned? It looked more
like shock to me!'

'You're being unreasonable, Cyn—'

'Probably because I *feel* unreasonable!' Cyn
gave another push against his chest with her bent
elbows, those tears still dampening her cheeks.
'So much has happened this evening that I—

Lucien, if you don't release me I'm going to start screaming, and I think the other guests staying at the hotel have already witnessed enough of a scene for one evening!'

'You're upset—'

'Of *course* I'm upset!' Cyn stilled to look up at him incredulously. 'I've just learnt that the friend I came to New York to visit has not only become involved in taking drugs, but has also been using me to hide his affair with another woman. Add to that the fact that the man I had dinner with and made love with earlier this evening also seems to have been involved with that woman—'

'I'm not involved with anyone but you.'

'I think that gives me the right to be upset, don't you?' she continued determinedly.

Lucien frowned his own frustration with the situation as he released her, before allowing his arms to drop slowly back to his sides, knowing he had handled this situation badly, that his first instinct—to kneel and worship at Cyn's feet— was the one he should have taken.

'I apologise. It— I— It isn't every day a man

learns that the woman he has just made love with is a virgin.'

'No, I believe we're becoming something of an endangered species.' She nodded abruptly. 'Thank you for the fun of cooking dinner together this evening, Lucien. I enjoyed it. The sex too. The rest of the evening... Not quite so much.' She stepped back. 'I'll make sure I have your T-shirt laundered and returned to you before I leave on Saturday—'

'Do you think I give a damn about my T-shirt?' he bit out in his frustration with her determination to leave him.

'Probably not.' She grimaced. 'I'm sure you have dozens of others just like it. Or you could *buy* another dozen like it! I would just feel better if I had this one laundered and returned to you.'

So that she didn't even have *that* as a reminder of him once she had returned to her life in London, Lucien guessed heavily.

Lucien wouldn't need anything to remind him of Cyn once she had gone.

He had spoken the truth when he'd told her that

he had been more open, more relaxed in her company, than he ever had with any other woman.

As for the sex...!

He'd had good sex in his life, pleasurable sex, and very occasionally mechanical sex, when mutual sexual release had been the only objective, but he'd never had such mind-blowing and compatible sex as he'd enjoyed tonight with Cyn, where the slightest touch, every caress, gave them both unimagined pleasure.

He had always believed that sort of sex had to be worked at, with the two people involved having a rapport that went beyond the physical to the emotional.

He and Cyn had something between them beyond the physical. Lucien had known Cyn a matter of days, and yet the two of them had instinctively found that rapport. In and out of bed. Only to have it all come crashing down about their heads the moment Dex rang to tell them of Miller's presence downstairs in the hotel reception area.

Not only that, but Cyn was a virgin, and now that Lucien knew that he realised that her shyness earlier was an indication that she was an inexperienced virgin. A *very* inexperienced virgin, who had climaxed half a dozen times in his arms. Which was surely unusual—and perhaps an indication that she felt more for him than just physical attraction?

Or was that just wishful thinking on his part...?

Lucien didn't know any more. Had somehow lost his perspective. On everything. A loss that necessitated in him needing time and space in which to consider exactly what he felt for Cyn. Time the mutinously angry expression on Cyn's face now told him he simply didn't have!

'Fine.' He tersely accepted her suggestion about returning the T-shirt. 'But I'll see you again before you leave—'

'I don't think that's a good idea.' She backed up another step, putting even more distance between the two of them.

Lucien scowled darkly across that distance. 'You're being unreasonable—'

'Outraged virgin unreasonable? Or just normal female unreasonable?' she taunted with insincere sweetness.

'Just unreasonable,' he grated between clenched teeth, not wanting to lose his temper and say something else he would have cause to regret. The fact that he was in danger of losing his temper at all was troubling. He *never* lost his control—let alone his temper. Tonight, with Cyn, he had certainly lost his control, and his temper was now seriously in danger of following it. 'You're putting words into my mouth now, Cyn,' he continued evenly. 'And we *will* see each other again before you leave. I'll make sure of it.'

She raised midnight brows. 'I'd be interested to know how.'

Lucien gave a humourless smile. 'I believe, ironically, that you're travelling back to London on Saturday on the Steele Atlantic Airline.'

'How on earth did you know that?' She stared at him incredulously.

'I checked.' He shrugged. 'I thought it would be a nice gesture to bump your seat up to First Class. Miller was a cheapskate for not booking you into First Class in the first place!'

'He did,' she snapped. 'I'm the one who insisted he change it to Economy.'

'No doubt because you have every intention of paying the money back to him.' Lucien sighed, only too well aware of Cyn's fierce independence. It was a knowledge that made his earlier comments—accusations!—even more ridiculous. And unforgivable.

'Of course.' She tilted her chin proudly.

Lucien nodded. 'Nevertheless, if you avoid seeing me again before you leave for the airport on Saturday, one telephone call from me and the flight gets delayed...or cancelled altogether.'

Cyn gasped. 'You wouldn't seriously do that?'

He raised a mocking brow. 'What do you think?'

'I think you're way way out of line on this—that is what I *think*!' she hissed forcefully.

He shrugged. 'Your choice.'

'You—you egomaniac!' Thia glared at him. Arrogant, manipulative, *impossible* ego-maniac!

Lucien gave a hard, humourless smile. 'As I said, it's up to you. We either talk again before you leave or you don't leave.'

'There are other airlines.'

He shrugged. 'I will ensure that none are available to you.'

She gasped. 'You can't do that—'

'Oh, but I can.'

Her eyes widened. 'You would really stop me from leaving New York until we've spoken again...?'

His mouth thinned. 'You aren't giving me any alternative.'

'We all have choices, Lucien.' She gave a shake of her head. 'And your overbearing behaviour now is leaving *me* with no choice but to dislike you intensely.'

He sighed. 'Well, at least it's *intensely;* I would hate it to be anything so insipid as just mediocre dislike! Look, I'm not enjoying backing you into a corner, Cyn,' he reasoned grimly as she glared at him. 'All I'm asking for is that we both sleep on this situation and then have a conversation tomorrow. Is that too much to ask?'

Was it? Could Thia even bear to be alone with him again after all that had been said?

Oh, she accepted that Lucien had been shocked at the way Jonathan had just blurted out her physical innocence. But Lucien's response to that knowledge had been—damned painful. That was what it had been!

'Okay, we'll talk again tomorrow.' She spoke in measured tones. 'But in a public place. With the agreement that I can get up and leave any time I want to.'

His eyes narrowed. 'I'm not sure I like your implication...'

'And my answer to that is pretty much the same as the one you gave me a few minutes ago— that's just too bad!' She looked at him challeng- ingly.

Lucien gave a slow shake of his head. 'How the hell did we get into this situation, Cyn? One minute I have my mouth and my hands all over you, and the next—'

'You don't,' she snapped, the finality of her tone implying he never would again.

Except...it was impossible for Lucien not to see the outline of her nipples pouting hard as berries against the soft material of his T-shirt. Or not to note the way an aroused flush now coloured her throat and up into her cheeks. Or see the fever-ish glitter in the deep blue of her eyes.

Cyn was angry with him right now—and justi-fiably so after his own train-wreck of a conversa-tion just now—but that hadn't stopped her from remembering the fierceness of the desire that had flared between them earlier, or prevented the re-action of her body to those memories.

'Tomorrow, Cyn?' he encouraged huskily. 'Let's both just take a night to calm down.'

She frowned. 'It's my last day and I'd planned on taking a boat ride to see the Statue of Liberty. Don't tell me!' She grimaced as she obviously saw his expression. 'You've never been there, either!'

He smiled slightly. 'You live in London—have *you* ever been to the Tower of London and Buck-ingham Palace?'

'The Palace, yes. The Tower, no.' She shrugged. 'Okay, point taken. But tomorrow really is my last chance to take that boat trip...'

'Then we'll arrange to meet up in the evening.' Lucien shrugged.

Cyn eyed him warily. 'You're being very obliging all of a sudden.'

He grimaced. 'Maybe I'm trying to score points in the hope of making up for behaving like such a jackass earlier?'

'And maybe you just like having your own way,' she said knowingly. 'Okay, Lucien, we'll meet again tomorrow evening. But I'll be out most of the day, so leave a message for me at the front desk as to where we're supposed to meet up.'

He grimaced. 'Not the most gracious acceptance of an invitation I've ever received, but considering the jackass circumstances I'll happily take it.'

'This isn't a date, Lucien.' Cyn snapped her impatience.

She was doing it again—making him want to laugh when the situation, the strain that now existed between the two of them, should have meant he didn't find any of this in the least amusing! Besides which, Lucien had no doubt that if he *did* dare to laugh Cyn would be the one throw-

ing potted plants around the hotel's reception—
in an attempt to hit him with one of them!

Just thinking of Miller's behaviour earlier tonight was enough to dampen Lucien's amusement. 'I want your word. I would *like* your word,'
he amended impatiently, bearing in mind Cyn's
scathing comment earlier about his always wanting to have his own way, 'that you will stay away
from Miller's apartment tomorrow.'

'I thought I might just—'

'I would really rather you didn't,' Lucien said
frustratedly. 'You saw what he was like this evening, Cyn. His behaviour is currently unpredictable at best, violent at worst. You could get hurt.
Far worse than just those bruises on your arm,'
he added grimly.

She looked pained as she shook her head. 'Jonathan's life is in such a mess right now—'

'And it's a self-inflicted mess. Damn it, Cyn.'
He scowled. 'He's already admitted he was only
using you as a shield for his affair with another
woman when he invited you to stay with him in
New York!'

'Even so, it doesn't seem right—my just leaving

without seeing him again.' She gave a sad shake of her head. 'I would feel as if I were abandoning him... Not everyone is as capable of handling sudden fame and fortune as you were,' she defended, when Lucien looked unimpressed.

'Damn it, Cyn.' He rasped his impatience with her continued concern for a man who didn't deserve it. 'Okay, if I see what can be done about getting Miller to accept help, maybe even going to a rehab facility, will you give me your promise not to go to his apartment tomorrow?'

'And you'll reconsider firing him from *Network*?'

'Don't push your luck, Cyn,' Lucien warned softly.

To his surprise, she gave a rueful grin. 'Okay, but it was worth a try, don't you think, as you're in such an amenable mood?'

Some of the tension eased from Lucien's shoulders as he looked at her admiringly. 'You are one gutsy lady, Cynthia Hammond!'

Thia was feeling far from gutsy at the moment. In fact reaction seemed to be setting in and she suddenly felt very tired, her legs less than steady. A reaction no doubt due to that fierceness of passion between herself and Lucien earlier as much as Jonathan's erratic, and...yes, she admitted *dangerously* unbalanced behaviour.

She was willing to concede that Lucien was right about that, at least; she had hardly recognised Jonathan this evening as the man she had known for two years.

But there were still so many questions that remained unanswered. The most burning question of all, for Thia, being the name of the woman Jonathan claimed to have seduced out of Lucien's bed.

Mainly because Thia simply couldn't believe that any woman would be stupid enough ever to prefer Jonathan over Lucien...

CHAPTER ELEVEN

'YOU JUST NEVER listen, do you? Never heed advice when it's given, even when it's for your own safety!'

Lucien's expression was as dark as thunder as he strode past Thia and into her hotel suite early the following evening, impressively handsome in a perfectly tailored black evening suit with a snowy white shirt and red silk bow-tie—making it obvious he had obviously only called to see her on his way out somewhere.

'Do come in, Lucien,' she invited dryly, and she slowly closed the door behind him before following him through to her sitting room. Her hair was pulled back in a high ponytail and she was wearing a pale blue fitted T-shirt and low-rider denims. 'Make yourself at home,' she continued as he dropped a large box down onto the coffee table before sitting down in one of the armchairs. 'And do please help yourself to a drink,' she invited.

He bounced restlessly back onto his feet a second later to cross the room and open the minibar, taking out one of the miniature bottles of whisky and pouring it into a glass before throwing it to the back of his throat and downing the fiery contents in one long swallow.

'Feeling better?'

Lucien turned, silver eyes spearing her from across the room. 'Not in the least,' he grated harshly, taking out another miniature bottle of whisky before opening it and pouring it into the empty glass.

'What's wrong, Lucien?' Thia frowned.

His eyes narrowed to glittering silver slits. 'You gave me your word last night that you wouldn't see Miller today—'

'I believe I said that I wouldn't go to his apartment,' she corrected with a self-conscious grimace, knowing exactly where this conversation was going now.

'So you invited him to come here instead?'

Thia sighed. 'I didn't *invite* him anywhere, Lucien. Jonathan turned up outside my door. You only just missed him, in fact...'

His jaw tightened. 'I'm well aware of that!'

She arched a brow. 'Dex?'

Lucien's eyes narrowed. 'It was totally irresponsible of you to be completely alone with Miller in your suite—'

'But I wasn't completely alone with him, was I?' Thia said knowingly. 'I'm pretty sure Dex followed me to the docks today, and that he was standing guard outside the door to this suite earlier. And no doubt he ratted me out by telephoning you and telling you Jonathan was here.'

Lucien's eyes glittered a warning. 'Dex worries about your safety almost as much as I do.'

'Who's watching your back while Dex is busy watching mine?'

'I can take care of myself.'

'So can I!'

Lucien gave a disgusted snort. 'I discovered the first grey hair at my temple when I looked in the mirror to shave earlier—I'm damned sure it's appeared since yesterday.'

'Very distinguished,' she mocked. 'But there

is absolutely no need for either you or Dex to worry about me,' she dismissed lightly. 'Jonathan only came by to apologise for the way he's behaved these past few weeks. He also said that when the two of you spoke earlier today you offered to give him another chance on *Network* if he agrees to go to rehab.'

'An offer I am seriously rethinking.'

She sighed. 'Don't be petty, Lucien.'

An angry flush darkened his cheeks. 'I made the offer because you asked me to, Cyn. Not for Miller's sake.'

'And because you know it makes good business sense,' she pointed out ruefully. 'It would be indescribably bad business for you to sack the star of *Network* when the programme—and Jonathan—are obviously both so popular.'

Lucien's mouth thinned. 'And you seriously think losing a few dollars actually *matters* to me?'

Thia slipped her hands into the back pockets of her denims so that Lucien wouldn't see that they were shaking slightly—evidence that she wasn't feeling as blasé about this conversation and Jonathan's visit earlier as she wished to give the impression of being.

She had seen Lucien in a variety of moods these past few days: the confident seducer on the evening they met, the focused billionaire businessman at his office the following day, playful and then seductive in his apartment yesterday evening, before he became cold and dismissive towards Jonathan, and then a total enigma to her after Jonathan deliberately dropped the bombshell of her virginity into the conversation.

But Lucien's mood this evening—a mixture of anger and concern—was as unpredictable as the man himself.

Her chin rose. 'I thought we had agreed to meet in a public place this evening?'

'I decided to come here after Dex called up to the penthouse and informed me of Miller's visit.'

'You could have just telephoned.'

'I could have *just* done a lot of things—and, believe me, my immediate response was to do what I've threatened to do several times before and put you over my knee for having behaved so damned irresponsibly,' he bit out harshly.

Thia frowned. 'Correct me if I'm wrong, but shouldn't *I* be the one who's feeling angry and upset?' she challenged.

Lucien's expression became wary. 'About what?'

'About *everything!*' she burst out.

He stilled. 'What else did Miller tell you earlier?' Lucien's expression was enigmatic as he picked up the whisky glass and moved to stand in the middle of the room—a move that instantly dominated the space.

'Nothing I hadn't already worked out for myself,' Thia answered heavily. She had realised last night, as she'd lain alone in her bed, unable to sleep, exactly who the woman involved in the triangle must be. There had been only one obvious answer—only one woman Jonathan had spent any amount of time alone with over the past few days. And it wasn't a triangle but a square. Because Simone Carew, Jonathan's co-star in *Network,* also had a husband...

And if, as Jonathan claimed, he had seduced Simone away from Lucien's bed several months ago, then Jonathan's assertion that Lucien, believing Thia was Jonathan's English lover, had seduced her as a way of getting back at Jonathan, it all made complete sense.

Painfully so.

Perhaps it was as well she would be leaving New York tomorrow, with no intentions of seeing Lucien or Jonathan ever again.

Not seeing Jonathan again didn't bother her in the slightest—they had said all they had to say to each other earlier.

Not seeing Lucien again—that was something else entirely.

Because Thia had realised something else as she'd lain alone in her bed the previous night. Something so huge, so devastating, that she had no idea how she was going to survive it.

She was in love with Lucien Steele.

Thia had heard of love at first sight, of course. Of how the sound of a particular voice could send shivers of awareness down the spine. How the first sight of that person's face could affect you so badly that breathing became difficult. Of how their touch could turn your legs to jelly and their kisses make you forget everything else but being with them.

Yes, Thia had heard of things like that happening—and now she realised that was exactly what had happened to her!

The worst of it was that the man she was in love with was Lucien Steele—a man who might or might not have been deliberately using her but who certainly wasn't in love with her.

'Such as?' Lucien prompted harshly as he saw the pained look on Cyn's face. 'Damn it, Cyn, even the condemned man is given an opportunity to defend himself!' he said as she remained silent.

She looked up, focusing on him with effort. 'You're far from being a condemned man, Lucien.' She gave a rueful shake of her head. 'And I think it's for the best if we forget about all of this and just move on.'

'Move on to where?' he prompted huskily.

She gave a pained frown. 'Well, Jonathan to rehab, hopefully. Me back to England. And you— well, you to whatever it is you usually do before moving on to another relationship. Not that we actually *had* a relationship,' she added hurriedly. 'I didn't mean to imply that—'

'You're waffling, Cyn.'

'What I'm doing is trying to allow both of us to walk away from this situation with a little dignity.' Her eyes flashed a deep dark blue.

'I don't remember saying I wanted to walk away.' He quirked one dark brow.

She gave a shake of her head. 'I know the truth now, Lucien. I worked out most of it for myself—Simone Carew. Jonathan filled in the bits I didn't know, so let's just stop pretending, shall we? The condensed version of what happened is that you gave Jonathan two separate verbal warnings, about Simone and the drugs, he invited me over here in an attempt to mislead you about his continuing relationship with Simone at least, and you—you flirted with me to get back at him for taking Simone from you. End of story.'

'That's only Miller's version of the story, Cyn…' Lucien murmured softly as he placed his whisky glass carefully, deliberately, down on the coffee table before straightening.

His deliberation obviously didn't fool Cyn for a

moment, as she now looked across at him warily. 'I told you—some of it I worked out for myself and the rest... It really isn't that important, Lucien.' She gave a dismissive shake of her head.

'Maybe not to you,' he bit out harshly. 'I, on the other hand, have no intention of allowing you to continue believing I have ever been involved with a married woman. It goes against every code I've ever lived by.' He drew in a sharp breath. 'My parents' marriage ended because my mother left my father for someone else,' he stated flatly. 'I would never put another man through the pain my father went through after she left him.'

Cyn's eyes widened. 'I didn't realise... Did your relationship with Simone happen *before* she married Felix?'

Lucien gave an exasperated sigh. 'It never happened at all!'

She winced at his vehemence. 'Then why did Jonathan say that it did...?'

'I can only assume because that's what Simone told him—probably as a way of piquing his interest.'

'I— But— *Why?* No, strike that question.' Cyn

gave an impatiently disgusted shake of her head. 'I've met Simone Carew a few times over the past few days and she's a very silly, very vain woman. So, yes, I can well believe she's capable of telling Jonathan something like that just for the kudos. It isn't enough that she's married to one of the most influential directors in television—she also had to claim to having had a relationship with the richest and most powerful man in New York!'

Lucien gave a humourless smile. 'I knew you would get there in the end!'

'This isn't the time for your sarcasm, Lucien.' Cyn glared. 'And if you knew she was going around telling such lies why didn't you stop her?'

'Because I didn't know about it until Miller blurted it out to me a few weeks ago.' He scowled. 'And once I did know it didn't seem particularly important—'

'Simone Carew was going around telling anyone who would listen that the two of you'd had an affair, and it didn't seem particularly important to you?' Cyn stared at him incredulously. 'What about her poor husband?'

Lucien gave a weary sigh. 'Felix is thirty years

older than Simone and he knew exactly what he was getting into when he married her. As a result, he chooses to look the other way when she has one of her little extra-marital flings.'

'Big of him.'

'Not really.' Lucien grimaced. 'He happens to be in love with her. And there are always rumours circulating in New York about everyone—most of them untrue or exaggerations of the truth. So why would I have bothered denying the ones about Simone and me? Have you never heard people say the more you deny something the more likely people are to believe it's the truth?'

'I wouldn't have!'

'That's because *you* are nothing like anyone else I have ever met,' Lucien dismissed huskily.

Thia didn't know what to say in answer to that comment. Didn't know what to say, full-stop.

Oh, she believed Lucien when he said he hadn't ever had an affair with Simone—why wouldn't she believe him when he had no reason to bother lying to her? It was totally unimportant to Lucien what *she* believed!

It did, however, raise the question as to why Lucien had pursued *her* so determinedly...

'What's in the box, Lucien?' Thia deliberately changed the subject as she looked down at the box Lucien had dropped down onto the coffee table when he first entered the suite.

'End of subject?'

She avoided meeting his exasperated gaze. 'I can't see any point in talking about it further. It's—I apologise if I misjudged you.' She gave a shake of her head. 'Obviously I'm not equipped—I don't understand the behind-the-scenes machinations and silly games of your world.'

'None of that is *my* world, Cyn. It's an inevitable part of it, granted, but not something I have ever chosen to involve myself in,' he assured her softly. 'As for what's in the box...why don't you open it up and see?'

Thia eyed the box as if it were a bomb about to go off, having no idea what could possibly be inside.

'It's a replacement for the blouse that was ripped!' she realised with some relief, her cheeks warming as she recalled exactly how and when her blouse had been ripped. And what had followed.

She couldn't think about that now! *Wouldn't* think about that now. There would be time enough for thinking about making love with Lucien, of being in love with him, in all the months and years of her life yet to come...

'Open it up, Cyn,' Lucien encouraged gruffly as he moved to sit down on the sofa beside the coffee table.

'Before I forget—I had your T-shirt laundered today—'

'Will you stop delaying and open the damned box, Cyn?'

'I can do it later,' she dismissed. 'You're obviously on your way out somewhere.' She gave a pointed look at his evening clothes. 'I wouldn't want to delay you any more than I have already—'

'You aren't delaying me.'

'But—'

'What is so difficult about opening the box, Cyn?' He barked his impatience with her prevarication.

Thia worried her bottom lip between her teeth. 'I just—I'm sorry if I'm being less than gracious. I'm just a little out of practice at receiving gifts...'

Lucien's scowl deepened as he realised the reason for that: Cyn's parents had died six years ago and she'd admitted to having no other family. And her relationship with Miller obviously hadn't been of the gift-giving variety—he was a taker, not a giver!

'It isn't a gift, Cyn,' Lucien assured softly. 'I ruined your blouse. I'm simply replacing it.'

A delicate blush warmed the ivory of her cheeks, emphasising the dark shadows under those cobalt blue eyes. Because Cyn hadn't slept well the night before?

Neither had Lucien. His thoughts had chased round and round on themselves as he'd tried to make sense, to use his normal cold logic, to explain and dissect his feelings for Cyn. In the end he had been forced to acknowledge, to accept, that there was no sense or reason to any of it. It just was.

There was now a dull ache in his chest at the

realisation he wanted to shower Cyn with gifts, to give her anything and everything she had ever wanted or desired. At the same as he knew that her fierce independence would no doubt compel her to throw his generosity back in his face!

Lucien was totally at a loss to know what to do about this intriguing woman. Was currently following a previously untrodden path—one that had no signs or indications to tell him where to go or what he should do next. Except he knew he wasn't going to allow her to just walk out of his life tomorrow.

He took heart from the blush that now coloured her cheeks at the mention of her blouse ripping the night before. 'I would like to know if you approve of the replacement blouse, Cyn,' he encouraged gruffly.

'I would love to have been a fly on your office wall during *that* telephone conversation!' she teased as she finally moved forward to loosen the lid of the box before removing it completely.

'I went to the store this morning and picked out the blouse myself, Cyn.'

She gave him a startled look. 'You did?'

'I did,' he confirmed gruffly.

'I— But— Why…?'

He shrugged. 'I didn't trust a store assistant to pick out a blouse that was an exact match in colour for your eyes.'

'Oh…'

'Yes…oh…' Lucien echoed softly as he looked into, held captive, those beautiful cobalt blue eyes. 'Do you like it?' he prompted huskily as she folded back the tissue paper and down looked at the blouse he had chosen for her.

Did Thia *like* it?

Even if she hadn't this blouse would have been special to her, because Lucien had picked it out for her personally. As it was, Thia had never seen or touched such a beautiful blouse before. The colour indeed a perfect match for her eyes, and the material softer, silkier, than anything else she had ever owned.

Tears stung her eyes as she looked up. 'It's beautiful, Lucien,' she breathed softly. 'Far too expensive, of course. But don't worry,' she added as a frown reappeared between his eyes, 'I'm not going to insult you by refusing to accept it!'

'Good, because it certainly isn't going back to the store, and it really isn't my size or colour.'

'Very funny.' Thia picked up the blouse carefully, not sure when she would ever find the opportunity to wear something so beautiful—and expensive!—but loving it anyway. 'I—there appears to be something else in the box...' she breathed softly as she realised the blouse had been hiding the fact that there was another article wrapped in tissue beneath it. 'Lucien?' She looked up at him uncertainly.

'Ah. Yes.' He looked less than his usual confident self as he gave a self-conscious grimace. 'That's for you to wear this evening—unless you already have something you would prefer. You looked lovely in the gown you were wearing the evening we met, for example, although you might feel happier wearing something new.'

Thia eyed him warily. 'And where am I going this evening that I would need to wear something new?'

'To a charity ball.' He stood up restlessly, instantly dwarfing the room—and Thia—with the sheer power of his personality. 'With me. It's the reason I'm dressed like this.' He indicated his formal evening clothes.

'A charity ball...?' Thia echoed softly.

He nodded. 'I thought we could spend a couple of hours at the ball and then leave when you've had enough.'

She looked at him sharply. 'Is this because of what I said to you last night?'

He grimaced. 'You said a lot of things to me last night, Cyn.'

Yes, she had—and quite a lot of them had been insulting. Most especially the part where she had suggested Lucien was hiding her away because he didn't want to be seen in public with a waitress student from London...'There's really no need for you to do this, Lucien. I was out of line, saying what I did, and I apologise for misjudging you—'

'You apologised for that last night,' he dismissed briskly. 'Tonight we're going out to a charity ball. Most, if not all of New York society will be there too.' Lucien met her gaze unblinkingly.

'Exactly how much per ticket is this charity

ball?' Thia had seen several of these glittering affairs televised, and knew that they cost thousands of dollars to attend.

'What the hell does that have to do with—?'

'Please, Lucien.'

His mouth thinned. 'Ten thousand dollars.'

'For *both?*' she squeaked.

'Per ticket.'

'Ten thous…?' Thia couldn't even finish the sentence—could only gape at him.

He shrugged. 'The proceeds from the evening go towards the care of abused children.'

Even so… Ten thousand dollars a ticket! It was—'I can't allow you to spend that sort of money on me.' She gave a determined shake of her head.

'It isn't for you. It's for abused children. And I've already bought the tickets, whether we attend or not, so why not use them?'

'Because—because I—' She gave a pained wince. 'Why don't you just take whoever you were originally going to take?'

'I bought the extra ticket today, Cyn. You *are*

the person I was originally going to take.' His gaze was compelling in its intensity.

Maybe so, but that didn't mean Thia had to go to the charity ball with him.

Did it...?

CHAPTER TWELVE

'THAT WASN'T SO bad, was it…?' Lucien turned to look at Cyn as the two of them sat in the back of the limousine, driven by Paul, with Dex seated beside him, and they left the charity ball shortly before midnight.

'It wasn't bad at all. Everyone was so…nice.' She looked at him from beneath silky dark lashes.

'They can be.' Lucien nodded.

'It probably helped that I was being escorted by the richest and most powerful man in New York!'

'I didn't notice any pitying glances being directed my way,' he teased huskily.

'If there were, they were kept well hidden!'

Lucien reached across the distance between them to lift up one of her hands before intertwining his fingers with hers—ivory and bronze. 'Will you come up to my apartment for a nightcap when we get back to the hotel?' he invited gruffly.

Thia gave him a shy glance in the dimly lit confines of the back of the limousine. The privacy partition was up between them and the front of the car. To her surprise, she had enjoyed the evening much more than she had thought she would, meeting so many more people than just the celebrity side of New York society. Such was the force of Lucien's personality that all of them had accepted her place at his side without so much as a raised eyebrow.

The only moment of awkwardness for Thia had been when they had spoken briefly to Felix and Simone Carew. The older woman had avoided meeting Thia's gaze—that fact alone telling Thia that Jonathan must have spoken to the actress today, and that Simone knew Thia now knew about the two of them.

Lucien's manner had been extremely cool towards the other woman, and his arm had stayed possessively about Thia's waist as he spoke exclusively to Felix, before making their excuses so that he could introduce Thia to some friends of his across the room. That arm had remained firmly about her waist for the rest of the evening.

She had even worn the gown Lucien had selected and bought for her. A bright red figure-hugging, ankle-length dress that left her shoulders and the swell of her breasts bare. And she had secured the darkness of her hair at her crown. The appreciation in Lucien's eyes when she'd rejoined him in the sitting room of her suite had been enough to tell her that he approved of her appearance.

She moistened her lips with the tip of her tongue now. 'Is that a good idea?'

His fingers tightened about hers. 'We can go to your suite if you would prefer it?'

'I've had a lovely time this evening, Lucien, but—'

'This sounds suspiciously like a brush-off to me.' He had tensed beside her.

Thia gave a shake of her head. 'I'm leaving in the morning, Lucien. Let's not make things complicated.'

His eyes glowed in the dim light. 'What if I want to complicate the hell out of things?'

She smiled sadly. 'We both know that isn't a

good idea. I'm…what I am, and you're…what you are.'

'And didn't tonight prove to you that I don't give a damn about the waitress/student/billionaire/businessman thing?'

Thia chuckled huskily. 'The difference between us I was referring to was actually the virgin and the man of experience thing!'

'Ah.'

'Yes—*ah*. A difference that horrified you last night,' she reminded him huskily.

'It didn't horrify me. I was just surprised,' he amended impatiently. 'But I'm over the surprise now, and—'

'And you want to continue where we left off last night?' Thia arched her brows.

'You know, Cyn, when—if—I've ever thought of proposing marriage to a woman, I certainly didn't envisage it would be in the back of a car. Even if that car *is* a limousine! But if that's how it has to be, then I guess—'

'Did you say you're proposing marriage…?' Thia turned fully on the leather seat to look at him with wide disbelieving eyes. Lucien couldn't really mean he was proposing marriage to *her*!

'Well, no,' he answered predictably. 'Because I haven't actually got around to asking you yet,' he added dryly. 'I believe I need to get down on one knee for that, and although the back of this car is plenty big enough I think you would prefer that Paul and Dex didn't make their own assumptions as to exactly what I'm doing when I drop down onto my knees in front of you!'

Thia felt the warm rush of colour that heated her cheeks just at the thought of what the other two men might think about seeing their employer falling to his knees in the back of the car.

She snatched her hand out of his. 'Stop teasing me, Lucien— What are you doing?' she gasped as he moved down onto his knees in front of her after all, before taking both of her hands in his. 'Lucien!'

What *was* he doing?

How the hell did Lucien know? He was still travelling that untrodden path with no signs or indications to guide him.

Thia had obviously enjoyed herself this evening, and he could only hope part of that enjoyment had been his own company.

She looked so beautiful tonight Lucien hadn't been able to take his eyes off her. The fact that other men had also looked at her covetously had been enough for Lucien to keep his arm possessively about her waist all evening, rather than just accepting the glances of admiration his dates usually merited. He didn't want any other man admiring Thia but him.

He knew it was probably too soon for Cyn. That the two of them had only known each other a couple of days. But what a couple of days they had been!

That first evening, when he had literally looked across a crowded room and seen her for the first time, she'd been so beautiful she had taken his breath away. And he had felt as if she had punched him in the chest later on, when she'd preferred to walk away from him, in the middle of a crowded New York street, rather than accompany him to Steele Heights Hotel. The following morning, when he had seen the disreputable hotel where she had spent the night, he'd actually had palpitations! And when she had arrived at his office later that afternoon, wearing that cropped pink T-shirt and those figure-hugging low-rider denims, his physical reaction had been so wonderfully different...!

Cooking dinner last night with Cyn had been fun, and their conversation stimulating, while at the same time Lucien had felt more comfortable, more at ease in her company than he had ever been before. And she had looked so cute in his over-sized T-shirt. He had even enjoyed shopping for the blouse and gown for her earlier today. As for making love with her last night... How Cyn had responded, the way she had given herself to him totally, only for him to learn later that she was inexperienced, an innocent, had literally brought him to his knees.

And he had been on his knees ever since.

He was on his knees again now...

'I'm really not insane, Cyn.' His hands tightened about hers as he looked up intently into her beautiful pale face. 'I am, however, currently shaking in those handmade Italian leather shoes you mentioned at our first meeting,' he admitted ruefully.

She blinked. 'Why?'

'I've never proposed to a woman before, and the thought of having you refuse is enough to make any man shake.'

Cyn gave a pained frown. 'I don't—this is just—'

'Too soon? Too sudden? I know all that, Cyn.' He grimaced. 'I've been telling myself the same thing all day. But none of it changes the fact that I've fallen in love with you—that the thought of you going back to London tomorrow, of never seeing you again, is unacceptable to me. I don't just love you, Cyn, I adore you. I love your spirit, your teasing, your intelligence, your kindness, your loyalty, the way you give the whole of yourself, no matter what the situation. I had no idea how empty my life and heart were until I met you, but you've filled both of them in a way I could never have imagined. In a way I never want to live without,' he added huskily.

Thia stared at him incredulously. Had Lucien just said—? Had he really just told her that he loved her? He adored her?

Maybe she was the one who was insane—because he really couldn't have said those things.

Not to *her*. Not Lucien Steele, American zillion-aire, the richest and most powerful man in New York.

And yet there he was, on his knees in front of her, her hands held tightly in his as he gazed up at her with such a look of love Thia thought her heart had actually stuttered and then stilled in her chest.

'Hey, look…you don't have to answer me now.' He'd obviously mistaken her look of disbelief for one of panic. 'There's no rush. I realise that it's too much for me to expect you to know if you'll ever feel the same way about me, but we can spend as long as you like getting to know each other better. You'll want to go back to London anyway, to finish your degree. I'll buy an apartment there, or maybe a house, so that we can spend as much time together as you have free, and then, after a few months, if you—'

'Yes.'

'If you still don't think you could ever love me the way I love you, then I'll—'

'Yes.'

'I'll somehow have to learn to accept it, to live with that. I won't like it, but—'

'I said *yes,* Lucien.' Thia squeezed his hands to pull him up so that she could look directly into his face. 'I said yes, Lucien...' she repeated softly as he returned her gaze questioningly.

'Yes, what...?'

Her breath caught in her throat, tears stinging the backs of her eyes. But they were tears of happiness. Lucien loved her. He really loved her. He knew that she had struggled to finance her degree and understood she was determined to finish it. He was going to buy a home in London so that he could be close to her while she did so. He had asked her to *marry* him!

Yes, it was too soon.

For other people.

Not for Lucien and Thia.

Because they were a result of their past—people who had both lost the security of their parents in different ways, at a vulnerable time in their lives. As a result they were two people who didn't love or trust easily—and the fact that they had fallen in love with each other surely had to be fate's reward for all those previous years of loneliness.

Thia slid forward on the leather seat and then down onto her knees in the carpeted footwell beside him. 'I said yes, Lucien.' She raised her hands to cup each side of his beloved and handsome face. 'Yes, I love you, too. Yes, I'll marry you. Tomorrow, if you like.'

'I— But—'

'Or maybe we can wait a while, if that's too soon for you. Lucien!' She gasped as he pulled her tightly against him before his mouth claimed hers hungrily.

'I'll take that as a yes to us getting married, then,' Lucien murmured a long time later, when the two of them were cuddled up together on one of the sofas in the sitting room of his penthouse apartment at Steele Heights, with only a side lamp to illuminate the room.

Cyn stirred beside him. 'I still think you're mean to make me wait for you until our wedding night.'

'Shouldn't that be my line?' he came back indulgently, more relaxed, happier than he had ever been in his life before. How could he feel any other way when he had the woman he loved beside him?

'It should, yes.' She pouted up at him. 'But you're the one who's gone all "not until we're married" on me.'

Lucien chuckled softly, trailing her loosened hair like midnight silk over his fingers. 'That doesn't mean we can't...*be* together before then. I would just prefer that we left things the way they are for now. I can't wait to see you walk down the aisle to me, all dressed in white and all the time knowing that I'm going to undress you later that night and make love to you for the first time.'

When he put it like that...

Cyn moved up on her elbow to look down at him, loving how relaxed Lucien looked, how *loved* he looked. 'What do you mean, we can *be* together before then...?'

His mouth quirked seductively. 'You enjoyed what we did last night, didn't you?'

'Oh, yes.' Her cheeks grew hot at the memory of their lovemaking.

'Would you like to repeat it tonight?'

'That depends...'

His smile faded to a frown. 'On what?'

Thia gave a rueful smile. 'On whether or not you'll allow me to...reciprocate. You'll have to show me how, of course, but I'm sure I'll quickly get the hang of it—'

'Dear God...!' Lucien gave a pained groan and closed his eyes briefly, before opening them again, those same eyes narrowing as he saw how mischievously she returned his gaze. 'You're teasing me again!' he realised self-derisively.

'Only partly.' She wrinkled her nose at him. 'I know the mechanics, of course, but I'm guessing that doesn't mean a whole lot when it comes to the real thing?'

'Let's go and see for ourselves, shall we...?' Lucien stood up, bending down to lift her up into his arms and cradling her tenderly against his chest.

Thia wrapped her arms about his shoulders and gazed up at him adoringly. 'I could get used to this.'

'I very much hope that you do—because I intend spoiling and petting you for the rest of your life.' That same love glowed in Lucien's eyes as he looked down at her. 'I love you very much, Cynthia Hammond. Thank you for coming into my life.'

Her lips trembled with emotion. 'I love *you* very much, Lucien Steele. Thank *you* for coming into my life.'

It was everything.

Now.

Tomorrow.

Always.

* * * * *